Strange Stories for Weird People

by

Scott West

Other books by Scott West:
Ghosts on the Highway

Sepulcro de Demonios was first published in the anthology *Corpus Pretereo*

Ashes to Ashes was first published in *Uncertainties III* by Swan River Press

The Monster in the Meadow was first published in the magazine *Tales of the Talisman*

Book design and artwork by Timothy Murphy
timothy.shane.murphy@gmail.com

ISBN: 979-8-218-32712-5

Quill & Ivy Publishing
Olympia, Washington

Contents

Introduction

Are you weird?

If so, these stories are for you. But they're also for me. Maybe mostly for me. See, I've been weird all my life and when I write, I'm writing the things I know I'd like to read about. It's not until the story is finished that I begin to wonder if anyone else might like it, too. If I've done my job correctly, you will.

When I decided the time was right to put out a collection of my short fiction, one of the things I knew I would have to do is write this introduction. It seemed daunting but necessary. But I also thought it might be fun. Being a huge Harlan Ellison fan, part of what I've always enjoyed about his books are the introductions. Man, Harlan just couldn't seem to help himself. All of his books have introductions. Some of his books have an introduction *and* introductions to each story. I think at least one of his books has an introduction *to the introduction.* Well, I'm no Harlan Ellison and I won't bore you with overly verbose deconstructions of what you are about to read, but I figured a little background on each story might be helpful and, hopefully, interesting. And don't worry—*no spoilers.*

But before we get to that, let's talk a bit about weirdness. (Feel free to skip this bit of bio if it's not your thing. I promise I won't be offended.)

I was a weird kid. I grew up in an era when things like comic books, horror movies and heavy metal were still relegated to freak show status by most of polite society. Now all that stuff is mainstream, and frankly the worse for it, in my opinion. I spent Sunday afternoons watching Sci-Fi Theater on KSTW, channel 11 and Friday nights watching Owl Theater on KCPQ, channel 13--both local Seattle-Tacoma affiliates, when there was still such a thing as local television. Sundays were for *Godzilla, The Thing from Another World, The Brain from Planet Arous,* and various and sundry insects made gigantic through the power of mishandled atomic radiation. Fridays were spent with my best friends, Dracula, Frankenstein's Monster, the Wolfman, Mummy, etc., in gothic black and white or garish technicolor, depending on if they were running a Universal or a Hammer horror film that night. I read stacks of Marvel comics (Bronze Age) and *Famous Monsters of Filmland Magazine.* When that illustrious periodical finally gave up the ghost, I picked up my first copies of *Fangoria* and *Starlog.* An early reader, I was always drawn to the strange and fantastic. Ray Bradbury was an early influence. Robert E. Howard's *Conan* stories fired my imagination. I read Alan Dean Foster's movie novelizations and then found out he also had many original books, which I sought out and read with delight. I came across my first Stephen King paperback in junior high, devoured it, and went searching for more. I discovered the rock group KISS in 4th grade and systematically worked my way from them to AC/DC, Motley Crue, Iron Maiden and then was introduced to a scrappy little foursome called Metallica, whose debut album *Kill 'Em All* blew my mind. From there I discovered Slayer, Venom, Voivod, Celtic Frost and on and on. Man, those were the days.

This little bit of biography is just to point out that while I was immersing myself in comic books, horror, science fiction and heavy metal music (and later, punk rock), most of my peers were doing things like playing sports and exploring the whole boy/girl dynamic. In high school they were attending homecoming and prom, aiming for first string on the football team or shooting at being head cheerleader, taking college courses in pursuit of academic achievement and doing it all to a background of Top 40 pop music and MTV. I was drawing monsters, dinosaurs, robots, and pentagrams in the margins of my homework and teaching myself to play guitar so I could escape my small town and become a rock star.

From 1st to 6th grade, I had exactly *one* real friend. He was weird, too. Then a kid as weird as we were moved in down the road and I had two friends, until my original friend moved away in 8th grade, and I was back down to one. I was more gregarious once I reached high school (not a lot, but more than I'd been previously), but as a kid I was alone a lot. I'm not complaining. See, what it did for me was it encouraged me to use my imagination. I fear that imagination is something that's sorely lacking, nowadays. And when I hear somebody self-deprecatingly refer to themselves as "weird", usually accompanied by a modest little laugh, because they like whatever blockbuster superhero movie is currently playing at the local theater (or, more likely, streaming), or they cosplay at the local MegaCon, I have to just shake my head. See, kids like me used to get picked on regularly for liking the stuff we liked. And I'm not talking about a little razzing. I watched in horror one time on the school bus as two older kids slapped my (one) friend around until he cried just because he was reading a *Sword of Shannara* fantasy paperback.

It didn't get easier, either. I chose the path of most resistance in high school by growing my hair long and doing my best to look like Ozzy Osbourne. Believe me, in a tiny rural Pacific Northwest town in those days, that was just asking for a fight. My friend, Rif, discovered punk rock in high school and did something even more radical than the three or four of us guys who dared to have hair past our shoulders; he shaved his head into a mohawk. Not just that; he also dyed it blue and red. He was hounded mercilessly and even got into physical altercations. Things were so bad for him he eventually split town and attended an alternative school. Rif was weird, and despite all the adversity, he wore it like a badge.

My little circle of friends in high school treasured horror movies and books, comics, science fiction, Dungeons & Dragons, heavy metal, punk, goth rock (those kids we called "bat-cavers", a way cooler moniker than just "goths", I think) and video games. None of which were considered mainstream at the time. And, yes, we were weird. But we were also free. And I wouldn't have it any other way.

Weirdness has been co-opted by the mainstream, kids. Let's take it back. What do you say?

To quote Joe Bob Briggs: We are the weird!

Now, the stories:

Tijuana Cockfight - This might be the most uncategorizable story in this collection. Even I don't know what compelled me to write a story about cockfighting—one of most repugnant activities one could ever engage in. And yet, one day when I sat down to write, this quirky bird and his female human friend showed up and demanded that I document their tale. Equally surprising was the appearance of Cheetah and Laredo, two colorful cowboy drifters who had wandered through several other of my unfinished stories. I guess they were pissed about my never seeing their adventures through to the end. Well, boys, you finally get to see print. Cheers.

Dark, Light, Dark - This one I consider to be a straightforward horror tale using the universal fear of the dark. I grew up in an extremely rural area and have vivid memories of losing our power during windstorms when I was a kid. My parents would light kerosene lamps and I'd huddle in a dark corner, listening to the wind screaming through the tall pines that surrounded our house. The flickering light from the kerosene lamps cast strange shadows on the walls that my vivid imagination would turn into the most unsettling images. I think those memories might have been the catalyst for this story.

The Pub - There comes a time when every writer of weird fiction must try their hand at an H.P. Lovecraft homage. Well...this is my time. *Cthulhu fhtagn*, motherfuckers!

Mr. 6 O'Clock - I believe children (and animals) have the ability to see beyond the veil of what we collectively agree to call "reality", and that that veil becomes heavier and harder to penetrate as we grow into adulthood. Although, I also think that it might come full circle in the end, in that the closer we come to leaving this world that veil once again becomes as gossamer, giving us a glimpse of...well, only those who have already passed through truly know. Anyway, all that is to say that when you're a little kid you can be aware of some extremely weird shit that would escape the attention of any adult. This story is about that. And the possible consequences of it.

Get Right with God - This is the most personal story in this collection and the most difficult to write an introduction to. It's a story about guilt and redemption—themes that seem to permeate a lot of my writing (see also The Pub, Winter of the Witch and Ashes to Ashes, as well as my novel, Ghosts on the Highway). Where does this come from? Well, like the main character of this story, I grew up a preacher's kid. This stuff is kind of hotwired into my psyche. However, I am not Nick, in case any of you get that idea. He is based on someone from my past, though; a family member who is no longer with us, due to a similar lifestyle. The choices I watched him make all through our childhood and early adulthood haunt me, because there is only the thinnest of lines separating us. I could have just as easily gone down those paths with him, and believe me, I took some steps in that direction. God only knows what pulled me back from the total darkness that he immersed himself in. Anyway, I am still here, and he is gone. Some of us live with our choices…and some of us die with them. RIP, man.

Thirteen Steps - Gritty, psychedelic, heavy metal horror. I took the premise from a Pacific Northwest urban legend, added a dash of 80s paperback original horror, a bit of 90s splatterpunk and a whole lot of anger and frustration and threw it into one of my favorite settings: the graveyard. I struggled with the ending to this one—I had the overall idea but couldn't think of how to properly wrap it up. The ending finally came to me fully formed in the shower one morning. Even so, getting it just right was an exercise in endurance and I almost gave it up several times. I'm glad I didn't. Just for fun, here is some of the music I was listening to while writing this story: Black Sabbath, Saint Vitus, The Damned, Coil, Bell Witch,

Bathory, Sisters of Mercy and Swans, among other dark and sinister artists.

Winter of the Witch - I'm fascinated by mythology, legends, and folktales. I also have a preternatural love for all things cryptid. So, this story's origin lies in my discovering a creature called the Waheela—a wolf-like monster that purportedly makes its home in Alaska and the Northwest Territories of Canada and wanting to write a story about it. That's it. That's all I had. As you'll see, this original barely-an-idea morphed into something completely different so that our monster ended up only a bit-player. Still, I rather like this story. I enjoyed writing in the voice of our young protagonist, Joe, and switching to grizzled old Grandpa Jake, neither of whom are actually anything like me. And maybe the Waheela will show up in another story sometime. He's still out there, you know.

Sepulcro de Demonios - This one is pure pulp and comes from my love of both low-budget horror flicks and Mexican Luchador movies of the 50s, 60s, and 70s. This story was previously published in the anthology "Corpus Pretereo" and was then adapted into audio form on The Lurking Transmission podcast, narrated by Jay Corso, which you can find wherever you prefer to listen to podcasts. It's also available on YouTube. The mastermind behind The Lurking Transmission is writer/musician Evan Dean Shelton and I highly recommend checking out his stuff. This is a dude that is not fucking around. Trust me, he's deadly serious and it shows. Jay is also an artist, and you should check out "The Plot", an animated short and web comic for which I voiced a couple of lines. As for the story itself, just kick back, pour yourself a shot of mezcal, and enjoy the ride. Larga vida el Lobo Gordo!

Ashes To Ashes - A few years ago I was asked by the writer Lynda E. Rucker to submit a story to the Swan River Press anthology "Uncertainties III", which she would be editing. I was honored and excited, but, man, was this one a lot of work. There was a very specific theme to the anthology, which I couldn't seem to stay within the bounds of, and, to the credit of Ms. Rucker and Swan River Press head honcho, Brian J. Showers, they worked with me until I finally shaped it into something publishable (although I think I still missed the mark as far as the Twilight Zone/Robert Aickman vibe they were looking for). It's still hard for me to believe that my work appeared in a hardcover anthology alongside literary heavyweight Joyce Carol Oates and one of my favorite 80's horror writers, Lisa Tuttle. The only downside is that I submitted one of the most embarrassingly overwritten biographies ever to see print. Oh well, lesson learned. Oh, the story itself? Yep, another guilt and redemption horror tale. But one I am pretty proud of.

The Monster in the Meadow - This is my first professionally published work and I still rather like it. I remember first submitting it to *The Magazine of Fantasy & Science Fiction* (start at the top, and work your way down, right?) and getting a hand-written response from then editor, Gordon Van Gelder. He liked the story okay but rejected it on the basis of it being too "Bradburyesque". Well, the rejection stung, of course, but the reason didn't. The story definitely and purposefully has Ray Bradbury's influence all over it. In my opinion, there is no finer world to inhabit than Ray's October Country and this story pays tribute to one of my all-time favorite authors, one of my biggest influences and that fantastic, perpetually autumnal world he created. It's also a tribute to friendship; specifically, the special bond you have with someone when you're very young. Bradbury explores this repeatedly, as does Robert R. McCammon in his wonderful book, "Boy's Life". Stephen King did it in "The Body" and other stories. This is my take; I hope you enjoy it.

By the way, several submissions later, "The Monster in the Meadow" was finally accepted by a fantasy/science fiction magazine called Tales of the Talisman. I can't remember how much I got paid for the story, but I do remember the physical check they sent me because it was emblazoned with the figure of Boris Karloff as Frankenstein's monster—the perfect first sale for a lifelong Monster Kid like me!

Alright, that's about all I have to say. It's time to let the stories speak for themselves. Let's get weird.

For Carolina, mi axo.

Simplemente destinado a ser.

Tijuana Cockfight

Lucy was on her way to Tijuana. Beside her, in a cage resting on the seat of the bouncing pickup, sat Pharaoh, her prize rooster. Pharaoh was calm, having been lulled to a near-hypnotic trance by the sound of the pickup's tires on asphalt—a sound he'd been listening to for over three days now. Or, somewhere in the dim recesses of Pharaoh's tiny birdbrain, he may have just been envisioning another glorious victory.

For Pharaoh was not a prize rooster in the 4H sense—no, he was Lucy's best and so far undefeated champion. He was the subjugator of the backroom brutality known as cockfighting—an illegal, but profitable, endeavor. The term "cocky" could have come directly from this bird, and Pharaoh seemed to know it.

Lucy had been driving from Washington State at a steady 90 mph since Monday morning. She figured it wouldn't be much longer until she hit the border. Turning up the radio, she began to sing along—off key and off time—to Marty Robbins's "El Paso," watching the dead, white sands and imploring arms of the saguaro roll by outside her window. She'd been listening to rock 'n' roll for most of the trip, but for the last half-hour or so all she'd been able to tune in on the ancient AM radio was country. Lucy didn't really mind—she wasn't a music snob.

"Pharaoh," she said, lifting her voice a little to be heard over the radio and the hot wind that blew through her open window. "You're gonna be world champeen, ya know that? You stick with me, kid." She chuckled to herself and patted the rooster's cage affectionately.

Pharaoh's eyes stared ahead, glassily.

Lucy exited Interstate 5 and headed down Highway 117 toward the Otay Mesa border crossing, still singing loudly along to the radio.

At the border, Lucy got out her wallet and calmly smoked a cigarette while she watched the border guards working over the line of cars in front of her. When it was her turn, she turned off the radio, stubbed out her smoke, and reached out a roll of bills to the guard before he could even say "Buenos días."

The guard took the money and glanced at the rooster in his cage then at Lucy. She pushed back her cowboy hat and pushed out her breasts so that they strained the material of her tank top. The guard's mustache twitched in what Lucy guessed must, for him, be a smile. He counted the money, stuffed the roll in his pocket, and waved her forward.

As soon as they were in Mexico, Pharaoh seemed to come out of his trance. He stretched his neck and ruffled his feathers. His comb seemed to stand a little taller.

Lucy rummaged through the glove compartment until she found a grimy, stained piece of paper. She pulled it out and tried to make out the fading pencil markings. She had written down the directions after six beers at The Roadhouse while waiting for a phone call from López. López's English was competent enough, but the connection was bad and the buzz in Lucy's head was good. She hoped she had understood the directions correctly.

Pharaoh began making strange hiccupping noises deep in his throat. This was a sign that he was sensing the impending fight. He could probably smell the blood of his opponent floating in the dry, dusty air. He raised his beak and snapped at the top of the cage, first drawing his neck down into his body and then releasing it like a spring-loaded javelin. Lucy reached under the seat and brought out a moth-eaten sheet emblazoned with images of Bugs Bunny and Elmer Fudd. She draped the sheet over Pharaoh's cage and the rooster settled down.

As she drove, Lucy thought about how she had gotten into this. At eighteen, her plans for her future had not included driving cross-country to participate in a cockfight—even one with a six-thousand-dollar purse. Yet here she was guiding her dilapidated pickup through the streets of Tijuana. Lucy shook her head in disbelief when she thought of the strange road she was traveling and how it had all been instigated by a simple fancy of her grandmother's.

First had come the dreams—her Grandmother Zooey insisting that the ghost of her husband, Rico, was visiting her. Rico was trying to tell her something, she was sure. Grandpa Rico who had been a boxing champion in the early part of the twentieth century. Grandpa Rico who had been killed in the ring but had died doing what he loved to do. At some point, Grandmother Zooey had decided that Grandpa Rico's spirit had returned to earth in the form of Pharaoh, who had a violent streak in him from the beginning. But, her grandmother insisted, he also had a sweet side as well and that was the telling point. Lucy humored her grandmother in this harmless fantasy for months until one day Grandmother Zooey approached her with Grandpa Rico's wish...to fight again.

At first, Lucy resisted, but her grandmother's nagging insistence eventually wore her down. Once begun, Lucy discovered she had an affinity for the sport, and Pharaoh seemed to take to her immediately. Sometimes he would look at her and she could imagine that maybe, somewhere deep down in those beady eyes she saw... Anyway, after their first match, Lucy and Pharaoh were inseparable. Grandmother Zooey was happy, and Lucy began a lucrative career as a cockfight trainer. She acquired a half-dozen more roosters and spent six months out of the year traveling around with her "boys." She had never traveled quite so far before, but she had never been offered six thousand dollars before either.

Lucy followed the directions until she found the place she was looking for—the Hacienda del Rio, a nice, clean-looking hotel in the Zona Río section of the city. Lucy was a little surprised (and just a bit disappointed) at the lack of tackiness and sleaze. Her expectations had been of a sinister city full of tequila-swilling pirates and crap artists, whores and crooked cops, shadowy knife-wielding punks and gun-toting desperadoes.

She pulled her pickup into a parking slot and killed the engine. The motor died with a grateful gasp and then the hot metal began ticking like a time bomb. Lucy took off her hat, pushed back her sweaty mass of blond curls, and surveyed the hotel's parking lot. She saw American tourists carrying luggage to and from the lobby, saw cavorting children being chased or ignored by tired-looking parents, saw dutiful hotel employees greeting visitors, and saw the man she was looking for.

López leaned casually against a wall of the Hacienda del Río. He was not inconspicuous; tall, devilishly handsome, and dressed in some kind of vintage rockabilly suit. Dark, Elvis-style sunglasses hid his eyes. A dense, luxuriant mustache drooped over his lip. His hair was a carefully combed mass of oily hills and valleys, swooped into a 50's style Duck's Ass.

"Hang tight, little dude," Lucy said to Pharaoh, still sitting in the dark under the Bugs Bunny sheet. "I gotta go talk to this guy, and then I'll be right back." She patted the cage and hopped out of the truck.

López turned idly and nodded almost imperceptibly to Lucy as she approached him. She began to speak and López lifted a finger to his lips, "Shhh."

He motioned her to follow him. They walked across the parking lot and López opened the passenger door of a sky-blue '78 Chevy Impala. Lucy looked inside skeptically. The floor of the car was covered with old, wadded-up newspapers and large paper cups, the kind you got at 7-11 or other convenience stores (Lucy wondered whether Tijuana had any 7-11's). Finally, she slid inside the car and López slammed the door shut and walked around to the other side. He got in next to Lucy.

"It's all set?" Lucy asked as soon as he had shut the door.

"Sí."

"Good. When and where?"

"Settle down, muchachita. There are other things we must discuss."

Lucy's eyes narrowed, "What other things?"

López unhurriedly picked up a crumpled pack of cigarettes off the dashboard, shook one out, and searched his pockets for a match. Lucy rolled her eyes with impatience. He struck the match on the exposed metal of the car's interior where a piece of vinyl covering had been ripped away. López lit the cigarette and inhaled deeply. As he spoke, a steady stream of bluish smoke trailed out from between his lips.

"Your opponent, he has brought a—how you say?—un impostor...a ringer."

"Ringer? What the hell are you talking about?"

López took another drag off his cigarette. "Un cabrón. Your gallo will surely be killed if you go through with this fight."

Lucy started to protest but López waved her off. "You must understand, Señorita Lucy, that I had no previous knowledge of this mañas...this trickery. I am as upset as you. My standing as promoter supremo is being seriously questioned at this time."

Lucy leaned back into the wide seat, frustrated with López's vagueness. "Look, dude—what do I have to do to get some straight information out of you? What are you saying? What's this about a ringer?"

López sighed with considerable emotion. He took off his sunglasses and his wet, red-rimmed eyes stared at

Lucy with compassion. "Your rooster, he will meet a mutante in the ring if you are foolish enough to allow this fight. Señor Guerrero's bird is not...natural. It is a freak! A travesty!" He rolled down his window and spat onto the pavement in disgust. "You should get back into your carro and go home, ve a casa, muchacha."

"I drove down here practically nonstop, you bastard!" Lucy bellowed. "On your word that this was a big deal! The biggest deal! Now you want me to go back home just because this guy has a weird bird? Forget it, López. What could be so bad about this bird anyway? Pharaoh can handle anything, man—anything. He's not afraid and neither am I."

López put his sunglasses back on, hiding his expressive eyes. "You should be," he said, before beginning to explain the situation. "Both of you should be."

When Lucy got back to her truck, she saw that Pharaoh had pulled the sheet most of the way off of his cage. He was still working at a corner of it with his beak when she slipped into the driver's seat.

"Shit, Pharaoh," she sighed. "We might have a teensy little problem, kid."

Pharaoh stopped nibbling at the sheet and stared at Lucy with deadpan eyes. Lucy started up the pickup and rolled slowly out of the parking lot and down the street. As she drove farther away from the touristy sections of Tijuana, she began to see the tacky, sleazy side of the town that she had envisioned. Dark, mysterious men loitered in the shadowy doorways of crumbling buildings. The sidewalks were cracked and dirty with weeds growing sparsely along the zigzags in the cement. Women with tight dresses and blank eyes strolled the streets, swinging their hips robotically. The sun beat down with unmerciful enthusiasm. Lucy felt beads of sweat rolling down her neck and chest.

"López says this guy has brought in some sort of twisted freak. I'm not entirely sure what he's talking about, but it sounds bad." She glanced at the rooster. "I don't know if we should risk it."

Pharaoh flapped his wings in agitation.

"I know, I know—you're a badass. You've beaten every bird you've gone up against since I got into this goddam game. But López thinks Guerrero has a..." She wasn't sure what to call it—López's English had failed him in the explanation. "A monster, I guess," she finished.

Lucy again tried to decipher what López had been trying to tell her. *Mutante*, he had said —something unnaturally born, but still a bird qualified to step into the ring and fight. Beyond that, she hadn't understood.

"I guess what I'm trying to say," she told Pharaoh, "Is that this one is up to you. What do you think, pal?" She stuck her finger up against the mesh of the cage and felt the rooster's beak tenderly nip her flesh. That was all. After that, Pharaoh settled into the corner of the cage and seemed to go to sleep.

Lucy sighed. He wants to go for it, she thought. Okay. Who am I to deprive him of his fun? She drove toward the edge of town and sundown.

Night fell on Tijuana, making the shadows that much more sinister. From her corner table in the cantina, Lucy carefully watched the bar's patrons from under the brim of her cowboy hat. She sipped at her beer, savoring the quick coldness running down her throat in the almost stifling heat. It seemed as if the air had turned even warmer since the sun had vanished below the horizon. On the floor next to Lucy's booted feet, Pharaoh sat quietly in his cage, covered by the sheet.

She glanced at her watch. Almost time.

Downing the last drops of beer, she threw a few coins on the table, grabbed the cage, and made her way along the wall to the door. She stepped out into the night, searching the street. Sure enough, at the next corner, López stood under a broken streetlamp, his arms folded over his chest. He still wore the sunglasses even though the sun had set. Lucy approached the promoter who, without acknowledging her, turned and began walking along the street. She followed along behind. Two blocks later, López disappeared into an alley. Lucy cautiously peered into the darkness and saw a single dim lantern burning above a sunken doorway at the other end.

"That must be it," she whispered to Pharaoh, still hidden beneath the sheet. Taking a deep breath and trying to ignore the sudden feeling of dread that was settling over her, she stepped into the alley.

At the bottom of the dimly lit stairway was a wooden door with a peephole at eye level. Lucy knocked on the door and the peephole slid open. A suspicious eye glared through it at her.

"Ve a casa, muchacha."

"¿Quién eres?", demanded a gruff voice.

"Fighter," said Lucy, holding up the cage. She pulled back the sheet and showed the eye of her rooster.

"Pásale."

The sound of bolts being unlocked could be heard on the other side of the door. Then it opened abruptly, and Lucy saw a large room. It was filled with shadowy figures and smoke swirled in the murky lantern light. She entered cautiously, feeling the staring eyes crawling over her as she headed toward the center of the room where a circular pit had been dug out and shored up with red brick. Around the pit men squatted, smoking, and taking long swigs out of a bottle of tequila that was being passed around. Most of the men in the room were Mexicans, but Lucy saw two who were obviously American. One was a lean, lanky cowboy wearing a checked shirt, cowboy hat, and scuffed boots and the other was a tall, burly-looking fellow with a boyish face. They appeared to be friends—or at least hanging out together. Lucy decided she would introduce herself to these guys after she talked to López.

López was casually strolling around the pit, talking to the contestants. He was arranging the order of the fights—matching up the opponents by size, experience, and whatever other criteria cockfighting promoters used. When he saw Lucy, he motioned her over. "Señorita Lucy," he said, "I was hoping you had gone back to your home."

"No way. Pharaoh and me are in it for the long haul."

"Well, then," López said, "I wish you good luck. You will fight Señor Guerrero in the third round." López disappeared back into the crowd, shaking his head.

Lucy wandered over to the two Americans she had seen previously. The smaller one was engaged in a heated discussion–in Spanish–with another man, so Lucy directed her remarks to the burly one. "Hey, man," she said, smiling, "I'm Lucy. Nice to see a fellow Americano here."

"Meetcha," said the man, tipping an imaginary hat. "Name's Laredo, that's my buddy, Cheetah," the big man said, inclining his head in the lanky cowboy's direction.

"You guys don't have a bird?" Lucy asked.

"Naw. We're just here for the betting." A sly look passed between the two men.

A cheer went through the crowd drowning out Lucy's response. The first match was about to get underway.

López escorted two men to the pit, explaining to them in rapid Spanish the rules of the fight. One man looked as if he was a farmer, dressed in a plain white cotton shirt and trousers and a straw sombrero; the other was tall and expensively dressed with a somber expression and an old scar that ran along his temple and down to his slightly down-turned upper lip; both men held covered cages. The men took up places on opposite sides of the pit when López finished with his instructions. They placed the cages inside, against their respective walls. López stood equally spaced between the two opponents, looking at his watch and moving his lips silently. Suddenly he lifted his head and shouted, "Our first contenders—El Demonio Sangriento contra Pájaro Fuerte! Comience!"

López stepped back from the pit.

The men each yanked away the coverings on their cages and with leather straps pulled up the cage doors. There was a roar from the spectators that was cut short by the appearance of the scarred man's bird. As it exited its cage an eerie silence filled the crowded room. The bird was ghastly—it looked like something from a David Lynch movie as scripted by H.P. Lovecraft and inspired by a Salvador Dali nightmare. The demonic bird lifted its misshapen beak and appeared to sniff the air. Then, in a blur of scales and feathers, it raced across the pit and took hold of the other bird's neck. There was a short squawk as its jagged beak clamped down on Pájaro Fuerte's throat and then the fight was over; the dead rooster's head dangled from the monstrous beak of El Demonio Sangriento while its body ran spastically around the pit, blood shooting from the ragged stump of its neck.

There was a chorus of “boos” from the crowd and the slap and jingle of money exchanging hands. A hail of peanut shells and bottle caps descended upon the pit and López angrily waved his arms in the air, yelling “¡Ya basta! ¡Párale!” at the agitated spectators. He signaled to a young boy who jumped into the pit with a garbage bag and with quick fingers cleared away the debris and then disappeared back into the shadows.

“Holy shit,” said Lucy, eyes wide with disbelief.

“That Guerrero’s a slick bastard,” said Laredo, who had watched the fight—all three seconds of it—next to her. His partner, Cheetah, took off his cowboy hat and swiped his brow with a faded red bandana. “Sucker breeds little monsters,” Cheetah said, replacing his hat. He pulled the hat down tight over his shaggy hair, adjusting the brim so that his sharp eyes were hidden in shadow. “Preternatural poultry, man,” he said, shaking his head. “López never should’ve allowed him in here.”

“It’s the money, man,” Laredo said, frowning. “Creeps like that always ruin the fun—they gotta turn ever’thing into a business.” He spat in disgust.

Lucy was only partly listening. Her mind was still trying to grasp the surreal scene she had just witnessed. She came out of her reverie with a start when she saw López coming around the pit. She grabbed his shoulders when he came within reach and shouted into his face.

"What the hell is that thing?!"

López shrugged off her hands, straightened his shirt and adjusted his glasses. "I tol' you, Señorita Lucy, but you no listen. I say Señor Guerrero's bird es un mutante, but you say you go ahead and fight. What can López do? Eh? Nothing." He passed his open palm between them, indicating his helplessness in the matter. "Your gallo will go up against El Demonio Sangriento after the next round. You should get ready."

López started to walk away, but Lucy stopped him once again. "You have Guerrero slotted for all three fights? Don't you think that's just a little presumptuous, not to mention preferential?" She was burning up with anger, her words coming out harsh and low through clenched teeth.

"Señor Guerrero's bird," López said, "he never lose." He shrugged simply and walked away.

During the pause between rounds Cheetah and Laredo excused themselves and went to a secluded corner to talk with another man. He seemed to be the owner of the rooster up for the next round—he held a caged bird loosely against his leg. She saw the man nodding and Cheetah and Laredo grinning. They bent down and appeared to examine the rooster. It took a peck at them through the cage wire and their grins grew even wider. The man slapped Cheetah on the shoulder and strolled over to the pit for last-minute preparations while the crowd busied itself placing final bets and trading shots of tequila.

The second round was over as quickly as the first. El Demonio Sangriento dispatched his opponent with gleeful ferocity, then lingered lovingly over the remains. Señor Guerrero beamed proudly at his freakish bird and allowed him to feast on the tattered remnants of the poor dead rooster, while López took the abuse of the crowd, both for allowing this monstrosity to fight and for not penalizing Guerrero for bad sportsmanship.

While they waited for the final round, Lucy and Pharaoh huddled together in a corner with their new friends.

"I don't get it," Lucy said, shaking her head. "What is it?"

"Chupachicken," Laredo said.

"Huh?"

"You ever heard of el chupacabras?" asked Cheetah.

"Nah. What's that?"

"Down here and in Central and South America there's this creature called el chupacabra...like a mythical beast, y'know? You got yer Loch Ness Monster over in Scotland, the Pacific Northwest has its Sasquatch—these places got their chupacabra. The name means "goat-sucker." They call it that cuz mainly they kill goats and drink their blood. Once in a while they get a cat or a baby or somethin', but mainly goats. Little buggers—look kinda like a cross 'tween a horny toad and E.T."

"Uh huh." Lucy looked doubtful.

"It's true," Laredo drawled. "My sister lives down in Del Fuego with her boyfriend, Miguel...they lost two burros to a chupacabra. It was goin' for a cow one night when Miguel blew it away. He kept the skin—what was left of it. I saw it myself."

Lucy lit a cigarette with shaky fingers. "So...what're you guys sayin'?"

"Guerrero, that sick bastard, somehow got one a them goat-suckers to breed with a chicken. I mean, what kinda sicko would do somethin' like that?"

Lucy stared at the nightmare that was Guerrero's bird. "You mean that ain't no real bird?"

"It's part bird," Cheetah said, "and part monster."

"Then why does López let him fight?"

"Guerrero's a big shot. He's got López in his pocket, along with half of Mexico."

"He's a scumbag," Laredo growled. "I owe him one for what he did to my sister—ooph!" Cheetah elbowed Laredo in the stomach and glared at him.

"Guerrero's not well-liked around here," Cheetah said, "but he's tolerated. He's got a lot of money, which translates into a lot of power. Lots of people owe him for some rotten thing or other. A lot of people would like to see him get it one time." He smiled grimly.

Lucy felt a tap on her shoulder. She turned and saw López gesturing toward the pit. "Is time, Señorita Lucy."

Lucy took a deep breath and steadied herself. She bent down to Pharaoh's cage. "Hey, little buddy," she said. "I'm sorry. I didn't know..." She lost the words and then decided there was nothing she could say that would make it alright for Pharaoh anyway.

Cheetah said, "Don't look so worried. Y'know, strange things can happen."

"That's right," Laredo added. "Never say die."

They walked away and Lucy saw them approach the man whose bird had been brutally eliminated and consumed in the second round. Then all three disappeared into the crowd. Across the pit, Lucy watched the madman, Guerrero, cooing to his monstrous hybrid. The "bird" still had blood matted and dripping from its disfigured beak. Its eyes were black and round and dull—they didn't even reflect the lantern light. Veins stood out on its scaly neck and Lucy thought she could see the beat of the thing's pulse. It was hypnotic.

She was pulled out of her rumination by López's shout, "El Demonio Sangriento contra Pharaoh! Comience!"

Lucy startled, pulled the sheet off of Pharaoh's cage and lost her grip on it, dropping it into the pit. She looked at López, but he gave no indication that the fallen sheet was a problem. She backed away and waited to watch her bird die. El Demonio Sangriento came out of his cage—but not like the first two times. This time the freakish fusion of bird and beast staggered through the hatch and stopped, looking dazedly around the pit. Its lump of a head swayed atop the muscular, scaled neck. Guerrero at first didn't notice his champion's odd behavior—he was turned around, smiling, flashing his gold rings and teeth at the unruly crowd. Pharaoh, however, took notice immediately. The big rooster dug his talons into the packed earth and set off at a tearing pace toward the monstrosity. El Demonio Sangriento took a shaky step and the leg collapsed underneath it. It opened its ferocious beak and let out a horrific hisssssss just as Pharaoh reached it. The rooster slashed a claw across El Demonio Sangriento's breast and blood blossomed across the feathery scales. The beast howled and hissed and struck out with its beak, but blindly, missing Pharaoh entirely. It managed to get its other leg working again and started to stand, but Pharaoh was there and stuck his beak like a spear into the mottled flesh of El Demonio Sangriento's meaty thigh. The monster thudded back into the dirt, moaning pitifully now. Pharaoh sensed imminent victory. Now Guerrero's attention was pulled back to the pit. He watched with wide, outraged eyes as Pharaoh's beak and claws plunged relentlessly into his mutant bird. Blood was pooling on the dirt and El

Demonio Sangriento was no longer moving except for occasional death twitches.

López declared the fight over and the crowd cheered with delight, many of them openly jeering Guerrero now. A raucous argument broke out between Guerrero and López in rapid-fire Spanish, which Lucy couldn't follow. But she was too amazed at what had just occurred to be much interested in the argument, anyway. She gathered Pharaoh back into his cage and tried to accept the friendly beating that the cockfight fans were now giving her as they surrounded her, pounding her on the back and saluting her with laughter and shots of tequila. At last, Guerrero spat in López's face with vehemence. López immediately signaled for two huge men who emerged from the shadows and picked Guerrero up bodily, escorting him out of the room. The young boy once again jumped into the pit and began cleaning up the mess that once was Guerrero's undefeated mutant.

When the crowd's celebration died down a little, Lucy excused herself from her exuberant admirers and collected her payment from López, then quietly slipped away into the night. She saw them through the window of the dark little cantina as she walked back to her truck—the two cowboys who had been at the cockfight.

Lucy entered the cantina and they both looked up from their beers as she stepped through the doorway.

"Well, looks like your luck held out," Cheetah said, nodding toward Pharaoh's cage.

"Yeah," said Lucy, seating herself in the booth next to the lanky man. "Damndest thing...that other fella's bird didn't even put up a fight. It came out and wobbled there like a drunk on a two-week binge, then Pharaoh laid into him, and it was over. Sucker never had a chance."

"Figured your bird was pretty good," Laredo said, sipping his Dos Equis. "That's why I laid a hundred bucks on 'im." He grinned. "Buy you a beer?"

Lucy chuckled and looked down at Pharaoh's cage affectionately. "I love this tough old bastard," she said. "He and I have been through a lot together. And I know he's about as badass as they come, but..."

"But what?"

"But I saw that thing tear up those other birds like they were nothin'. That thing was pure beast. I know Pharaoh should've been a goner."

A meaningful look passed between the two men. Cheetah stretched and said through a casual yawn, "Maybe that damn mutant got sick."

"Yeah," agreed Laredo, chuckling, "maybe it was somethin' it ate."

Both men broke into laughter as Lucy scowled, puzzled. Another figure stepped through the doorway, and in the brief illumination, Lucy recognized the owner of the second rooster—the one whose bird was not only destroyed but also partially eaten by El Demonio Sangriento. The man came over to the table and spoke quietly to Cheetah who responded in fluent Spanish. They talked so softly that Lucy could hardly hear them.

Then the two men shook hands and Lucy saw the little Mexican slip something into his pocket as he left the cantina. Cheetah leaned back into the booth and another of their significant glances passed between the cowboys.

"Okay, what the hell?" Lucy exclaimed. "You guys gonna let me in on it?"

"In on what?" Cheetah said, innocently. "Juan just happens to be a good friend of ours. I told him where we'd be after the match—just wanted to offer our sympathies for his loss, that's all."

Lucy's suspicions wouldn't be assuaged so easily. "That guy's bird...that mutant thing ate it!"

"Yeah," said Laredo, "Guerrero's been known to let his freak gnaw on an opponent or two—pisses the crowd off to no end. That's why he does it, though. Too bad it had to be Juan's bird this time—he's not very careful about what he feeds his birds sometimes, you know.

"That's right," Cheetah added. "That guy's careless, those chickens are apt to wander all over the place eatin' God knows what. I mean, any chicken feed that might've been—I don't know...contaminated, let's say—ol' Juan just leaves it lyin' around for any of them chickens to get into."

"That's just like Juan, too—to have contaminated chicken feed around in the first place," Laredo said, nodding.

"Yeah. Real irresponsible guy, that Juan," finished Cheetah.

Lucy was starting to get the picture. She let Laredo buy her that beer and when the waiter brought her the bottle, she held it up and said, "Here's to Careless Juan and his irresponsible ways." The two cowboys clanked their beer bottles with Lucy's, and they all took a swig. Lucy looked at Laredo over the rim of her Dos Equis. "That Guerrero must've really done something nasty to your sister. Remind me never to piss you off, man." Laredo just smiled to himself and sipped his beer.

Under the table, in the dark of his cage, underneath the Bugs Bunny sheet, Pharaoh nestled his head in his wing and dreamed of the ring and the thrill of victory and of a young, admiring Zooey.

Dark, Light, Dark

Doris locked the door to her flower shop and stepped out onto the sidewalk. She stood beneath the theater marquee and watched the sky turn from gold to purple like a seeping bruise. Tapping her foot impatiently as the theatergoers passed her by, she hugged her coat tighter against the autumn chill, searching the street for her ride. Cars drove slowly past, their headlights glowing in the dusk. Ten minutes passed. Traffic thinned out. Eventually, Doris stood alone in the circle of light cast by the marquee.

Her cell phone chirped and she fumbled in her purse for it, almost missing the call.

"Hello?"

She listened to the voice on the other end, her face registering impatience, then worry. Her sister, Maureen, would not be able to pick her up after all.

"But..."

Around her the night continued to darken. Someone inside the theater turned off the marquee and left her standing in the pale light of a quarter-moon. Half a block away the orange glow of an arc-sodium streetlight stood against the sky like a beacon. She fastened her desperate eyes on it while the voice on the phone continued to explain why she would have to walk home. Alone. In the night. In the dark.

"Maureen, you know how I feel about...yes, of course...the children come first, I know." She half-listened to her sister's explanations and apologies, watching the streets get darker and lonelier. A cold wind blew bits of paper and dust across the sidewalk, and she stared at her feet as Maureen made a final suggestion. "No, that's alright. By the time you got here I'd freeze to death." Doris stared at the streetlight and resolved not to be a bother. "It's fine, Maureen. You take care of the kids and I'll walk home. Just leave the porch light on for me, will you?"

Doris switched off her phone and replaced it in her purse. She took a deep breath of the chilly night air and began to walk home to the house she shared with her sister. Silently, she berated Maureen for abandoning her even though she was fully awarc of Doris's fear of the dark. In the city she would have been able to get an Uber or Lyft driver to take her home, but here in Spurgeon Creek there were no such amenities. No bus lines, no taxis. You either drove, rode a bicycle, or walked.

Doris used the streetlight as a destination, each step bringing her farther from the darkness and closer to the light. Once she had reached that first marker, she sighted the next streetlight, two blocks away, focused on it and began to move.

In this manner, Doris managed to reach the outskirts of town with only some minor anxiety, although she could feel her heart pounding within her chest. But now she was faced with the daunting prospect of leaving the relatively populated downtown area for the dark and quiet suburban neighborhoods where the houses were spaced far apart and hidden by scrappy pine trees and blackberry brambles. And the streetlights became fewer and farther between. Quietly humming a distracting tune, Doris stepped off the sidewalk and crossed an intersection to the waiting, unlighted, street corner. She desperately kept her eyes fixed on the upcoming streetlight, far off on the next block. Around her, the night closed in. The sounds of the town dwindled and were replaced by the chirping of crickets and croaking of frogs. A few houses had dim porch lights or the soft, blue glow of television sets in their windows behind pulled curtains, but most were dark and still. Doris huddled deeper into her coat as she hurried through the dark, shadowed spaces between streetlights.

At the corner of 9th and Fir Street, Doris hesitated. The quicker way home was to the left, but that way lay in almost complete darkness, illuminated only in a ghostly wash of the reluctant moon. Straight ahead, she could see the next streetlight, and, although it would add a few blocks to her trip, Doris decided to go toward the comforting orange glow. She crossed the intersection and increased her pace as she made for the next beacon, but as she approached her steps faltered, for underneath the streetlight a small, shadowy form leaned against the pole. Since leaving the downtown area, Doris had not seen any other pedestrians and this figure startled her. Its face was hidden in the shadow of a large-brimmed hat as it leaned nonchalantly against the post. Doris stopped, her breath catching in her throat. The figure gave no indication that it had seen her. She silently turned around and went back to 9th and Fir, and waited, not wanting to turn toward the darkness. As she looked over her shoulder, she took out her cellphone intending to dial Maureen's number. A message on the screen read *No Signal.* Apparently, she was in a dead zone. Behind her, the area underneath the streetlight was clear. Whoever had been leaning against the post was gone.

Doris debated whether to go back and turn on Fir or keep heading down 9th, which was the more lighted way. Now that no one was loitering underneath the streetlight it seemed more appealing to keep to the light, so she retraced her steps, this time making it all the way to the next corner, where she stood bathed in the orange glow, trying to calm her mind.

Ever since childhood, Doris had been afraid of the dark. It stemmed from the night of the biggest windstorm the area had ever seen. It knocked out the power for miles around, plunging every home into darkness. Eight-year-old Doris spent most of that night shivering under her sheets, listening to the storm rage outside, the wind screaming and causing the trees to lash their house with the violent tossing of branches. She remembered hearing voices underneath the howl of the wind and not knowing where they were coming from. Once, sometime during the night, she peeked out from beneath the covers and saw a light in the hallway. She immediately thought that the power had been restored but then realized the quality of the light was different from the electric lights she was used to. It reminded her of the Jack O' Lanterns they put out on their porch every Halloween. The light flickered in the hallway, an unstable, orange glow—dark, then light, then dark...

Shadows stretched along the hallway; long, distorted parodies of human anatomy. Whispered words she could not make out under the relentless barrage of the wind. And that orange, flickering light that made those terrible shadows dance.

Then the light was snuffed out and she was left alone in the dark, too scared to scream for her mother or father or even Maureen, in the next room. Just before the darkness, she thought she saw the shadows coalesce into a small form that leaned companionably against her doorway, accompanied by a soft chuckle that somehow cut through the horrible howl of the wind and the terrible, whispered words *I am waiting for you, Doris. In the dark. Always waiting. And I will get you.*

The next thing she knew, Doris somehow found her voice and she was screaming. Her mother and father were there, holding her, smoothing her sweat-slicked hair, telling her everything was okay, the storm was over, and everything was fine. Morning sunlight streamed through the windows. She stopped screaming and looked around. Maureen stood in the doorway; her face scrunched up with worry.

Since then, Doris had avoided the dark. In the evenings, when she locked up and left work, she always cast an envious glance at the people leaving the theater next door. Doris had never known the pleasure of seeing a movie on the big screen. Because theaters were dark. And the darkness was where he was waiting...

A dog's bark brought her back to the present. When she realized what she was doing, Doris, with a great effort, once again shoved the memories to the back of her mind. She sighted the next streetlight and quickly walked toward it. By the time she reached it she was almost running. Around her, the neighborhood was dark and silent except for that dog barking in someone's backyard. The quarter-moon was just a gray smudge behind deepening clouds. The next streetlight was two blocks away. Doris checked her phone—still no signal. How could Maureen do this to her? Consoling herself with the weeks of payback she would extract from her sister when this was over, Doris stepped off the curb and jogged toward the next light.

Halfway there, the light went out.

She stopped dead, panic flooding through her body. Desperately, she tried to adjust her vision to the darkness. Off in the distance she could see a pinpoint of orange light—the next streetlight, two blocks away. She ran toward it, tripping on the curb and falling to the sidewalk. Pain joined panic as her bare hands were scraped raw and one knee connected solidly with the concrete. She immediately got up and tried to run but could only manage a sort of hobble. She felt blood on the palms of her hands and tried to wipe them on her pants, but it hurt too much. Now there was no moon, no porch lights and no windows reflecting any light at all. Just the ball of orange light getting steadily larger. She kept her eyes glued to it and tried to ignore the pain in her hands and knee. Just a few blocks and she would be at home. All she needed to do was to continue playing this game of connect-the-dots with the streetlights. She was almost there. She stepped up on the curb under the streetlight and immediately it, too, went out.

Once again Doris stood alone in darkness.

Her mind was whirling.

Doris fought back tears as the panic surged through her once more. In the distance, a dim light could be seen through the overhanging branches of a tree—the next streetlight. She judged she was only about ten minutes from their house. Ten minutes—surely, she could keep it together that long, even in darkness. She moved forward once again, slowly this time, determined not to fall and do more damage to herself, but more just to prove to herself that she could keep her wits in this situation. But as she neared the next light, the shadows of the tree branches swaying in the breeze playing across it, blotting it out entirely for seconds, stopped her. The sound of the branches scraping against her window and the shadows slithering across the walls of the hallway as she huddled beneath her sheets came screaming back into her mind. Somewhere in the night she thought she heard laughter. Doris looked around frantically, but her eyes could not penetrate the shadows. She ran again, not caring about anything except escaping the darkness. Just as she stepped across the curb under the streetlight, she saw the shadow emerge from behind the tree. She stopped dead in her tracks. The shadow leaned against the tree, chortling softly from somewhere within. Certainly not from its mouth as under its hat it had no face. This time Doris screamed, no longer able to control the panic and terror. She ran, ignoring the pain in her knee. Instinct carried her toward their house. There were two more streetlights in the four blocks before she would reach Maureen's house. She was very close now, although time and distance had ceased to have any meaning for her.

The first streetlight went out before she even reached it. This time she did not even stop but sighted the next light off in the distance and kept running. Beyond that, some still-rational part of her mind realized that she would be only another twenty or thirty yards from the safety of her sister's home. She ran through the darkness, still hearing the heinous laughter in her head, still feeling the shadows following her, slipping toward her. She thought she felt a soft tickle behind her ear and screamed again, still running...

* * *

Maureen thought she heard a scream outside. She quietly left the bedroom where her three-year-old twins lay sick with fever and went to the front door. She parted the curtain and peered outside. The night seemed darker than usual. She flicked on the porch light, realizing that in her worry over her children she had forgotten to give Doris even that tiny bit of comfort. Down the road she saw that only one streetlight was working, casting a circle of orange, a halo of moths fluttering about it. Into that circle of light her sister, Doris, appeared, running full tilt. Doris opened her mouth, and another scream began but just then the streetlight went dark, and the scream was cut off in mid-voice. Maureen threw open the door and ran out onto the porch, searching the darkness. A moment later the streetlight snapped back on. She heard the hum of electricity, saw the moths gather around it once more, but her sister was nowhere to be seen. As she stared into the night, Maureen thought she heard someone chuckling softly.

She was still staring into the darkness, yelling her sister's name, when the porch light went out.

The Pub

Robert Morley sat drinking from a pint of lager and staring with red, swollen eyes through the smoky haze of the pub. He lifted the glass with a slightly trembling hand and drank noisily, leaving a froth of foam on his unshaven upper lip. The beer hit his belly like a bomb and spread its numbing aftermath through his body. A frown formed on his haggard face as he noticed the room waver and the shadowy faces of its patrons change.

It was Morley's first time in the pub—a dark, secluded shack at the water's edge, where waves lapped hungrily at the decaying foundation and the lights of a city could be seen from the other side of the broad, mysterious cove. It was a cold autumn night, typical for that time of year on the Olympic peninsula. Morley, a native of the Pacific Northwest, had dressed in a heavy sweater and olive-drab flannel jacket but could not seem to shake the chill from his body.

For weeks now, Morley had been drinking his way north heading toward this destination, guided by instinct like a spawning salmon. He was in no hurry, though, staying on for days in whatever town he happened to find himself in, getting blackout drunk until he'd worn out his welcome in every bar that town had to offer. Now he was continuing his bender here, in this town whose name he did not even remember, on the south end of Puget Sound. Even so, it was familiar to him. After all, this was where the most tragic event of his life had taken place.

The smoke that filled the room swirled languorously, and Morley was momentarily disoriented, thinking he was underwater. The round white faces of the pub patrons did not help any either, with their bulging bulbous eyes and slack sagging cheeks. They swam slowly through the smoke and dim lamplight, lipless mouths opening wide to gulp down their dark foamy beer.

Morley shook his head. "Need air," he muttered to himself. "Seein' things again." He got up too quickly, upsetting his table, knocking his glass to the floor. Pale faces turned in his direction, pints half lifted, as their watery eyes followed him. Morley stumbled to the door and pushed past a heavily bundled couple that was just entering. "'Scuse me," he mumbled as they turned their large, circular eyes on him, giving him room. Once outside, he leaned against the side of the pub and watched his breath puff out in great white billows.

The sign above his head, creaking in the strengthening wind, caught his attention. It was large, wooden, and hung by chains from a thick, splintery beam with the pub's name painted on it in Old English-style lettering. When he had first come across the pub, Morley had thought the sign said, "Dragon's Inn", but now, up close, he realized his mind had added a letter to a strange and unfamiliar name. Beneath the name, a painting of something—Morley squinted his eyes to bring the image into better focus—vaguely resembling some tentacled denizen of the deep, yet possessing some human qualities as well, making it strangely repulsive.

"Weird name," whispered Morley into the chill, briny air. "What does it mean?" Around him, the cries of seagulls mixed with the steady pulse of the waves and

Morley was suddenly overcome with a feeling of abysmal loneliness.

He pushed open the pub's door once again and stumbled inside, making his way slowly to the bar. He leaned heavily against the counter and breathed in the smoky warmth, unaware of the wide, unblinking eyes that turned his way. He crawled up onto a bar stool and held his head in his hands to stop the spinning.

"Help ya?"

Morley looked up and saw the bartender, a large, hairy man with a sloping forehead—as seemingly out of place here as Morley was himself.

"A pint of lager, please," Morley said quietly. He could see now, in the mirror behind the bar, the pale faces staring at him.

"Coming up," said the bartender, turning to the taps. He kept his half-lidded eyes on Morley as he drew the pint. When he set the glass down in front of Morley he said, "How'd you come to find this place?"

Morley looked up and saw genuine curiosity in the man's eyes. "I was just out…walking. I like to walk. Especially at night. Especially near the water." He took a large gulp of beer, wiped his mouth shakily.

The bartender began casually swabbing the countertop with a rag. "Like the water, do you?" he said. "Well, maybe you came to the right place after all."

"What do you mean?" asked Morley.

"You've really no idea about this place, have you?"

Morley glanced once again, quickly, into the mirror. Faces, round eyes, partially obscured by smoke and shadows stared back at him. He shook his head.

"No," he said. "You see, I...I guess I've been drinking a lot lately. I have trouble remembering things." He glanced uneasily into the mirror again. "My family...my wife and daughter...they were killed a while back. It was an accident, but..." He stopped, looked up pleadingly. It was the most he has spoken to anyone in weeks.

"That's pretty rough," said the bartender with sincerity. He nodded toward Morley's pint. "That one's on the house."

Morley nodded, sipped his beer. Turning around on the bar stool he noticed that the pub patrons had all gone back to their own conversations and concerns. He stared through the window at the sea, watching the dark waves roll to their own inexorable rhythm. The wind was building, and the salty foam flecked the windows as the waves crashed, louder now, against the pilings that supported that side of the pub.

"A lot of people here, they'd understand what you're going through," said the bartender, startling Morley from his reverie.

"Would they?" he asked with a trace of bitterness.

"Sure, they would. Maybe not exactly—everybody's pain is a little different—but enough to sympathize."

Morley sat up straighter, pushed his beer away from him. "I'm not looking for sympathy," he said, an edge in his voice.

"You're looking for something," said the bartender. Morley waited for him to say something more, but he turned to the taps and began polishing them with his rag. As he watched the bartender, Morley's ears picked up faint threads of whispered conversation.

"Look at the way the waves come crashing now. The Deep Ones are restless tonight for sure."

"When he come to be called to the Esoteric Order, all that changed, you can be sure. And I'll tell you another thing..."

"There's the new ones to initiate tonight, you know."

"And to think it falls on the anniversary of Cap'n Marsh's own calling to the Esoteric Order."

Morley sipped his beer and listened to the wind strengthening outside, whipping the waves into wilder heights. Something about the voices he heard struck him as strange and when it came to him through the fog of his increasing inebriation he beckoned to the bartender. The man ceased his polishing and leaned toward Morley.

"These people," Morley said softly, "they all seem to have New England accents."

The bartender nodded. "Yes, the majority of our patrons are displaced New Englanders. Although a more accurate term might be *persecuted*." He shook his head sadly and his mouth formed a grim line.

"Persecuted?" Morley asked.

"Religious persecution," said the bartender. These people live in a religious community of their own. Sort of like the Quakers or the Amish, you might say. Originally, it was a small fishing village on the coast, back east—a very tight-knit community. Most of these people are descendants of the founders of that village and of the village's religion. Eventually, they were run out—persecuted, as I've said—and the village was ultimately just...swallowed up by the sea."

"That's awful," said Morley, more than a little fascinated by the tale. The bartender just shrugged and turned toward the window, watching the dark, rolling waves. "So, these people just picked up stakes and moved out west?"

The bartender nodded, still staring out the window. "Yes. It was by an almost unanimous vote that they decided to relocate here in the Pacific Northwest. It was a long, hard journey for most of them but worth it, they felt, for the relative obscurity they could find here. You understand, this was in the 1940s, and this region was not too heavily populated—especially areas like this. Mostly small fishing towns widely spaced along the coast and around the inlets. Only a couple of big cities and those not so big, really, when compared to others back east. And they're an insular group. Keep to themselves, mostly, which is why they retain the accent."

Morley drank deeply of his beer and listened to the wind for a moment. He felt the dizziness hit him again and the room swam before his eyes, causing the faces in the mirror to waver. They looked almost predatory and full of shadows. A question came to him regarding the bartender's story, and he shook off the dizziness, lifting a shaky finger in the direction of the man.

"If all they wanted was to find a place to live in peace, why didn't they stop in Nebraska or Kansas or Montana, or…well, anywhere wide open like that? Hell, the Mormons planted themselves in Utah."

The bartender fixed him with a steady gaze. "As I said, it was a fishing village. It was a way of life for those people—the only life they knew or wanted. Can't you understand? Can't you hear the waves out there now, reaching toward us? You said yourself; you especially like walking by the water. Why is that? Could it be you sense the ancient kinship we share with those of the deep? When you stand all alone on the shore, don't you feel the rolling of the tide corresponding with the beating of your heart?"

Morley's head was spinning again. In the mirror the faces seemed to swim closer through the murky depths of the pub. The bartender's voice was strangely compelling, his words spoken with a quiet intensity. Morley looked down and saw that his glass was empty.

A hand touched his shoulder and he jumped. In the mirror he saw the people gathered behind him now; saw the flaking scales on their faces; the membranes stretched between the fingers of their cold, white hands; the wet, palpitating diagonal slashes on either side of their necks, just below the jawbone. Their round-eyed stares nailed him to his seat. He shook with sudden fear but could not move.

"You should consider joining them," the bartender said softly. "I have. Soon I'll begin the change, to be like them. You could too. You obviously have nothing else. Your wife and daughter...dead, as you said. You walk and you drink, and you live your life alone. I'm right, aren't I? Here, you could have a family again. Here you would not be alone. You would be a part of something bigger—something ancient that sleeps in the deep but will soon awaken."

Morley tried to stand and almost fell from the stool. His head was spinning, spinning. He looked in horror at his empty glass, at the knowing face of the bartender. He felt the hands gripping him tighter. The faces of his wife and daughter surfaced in his mind, washed ashore by the sea of memory. He opened his mouth to scream but no sound emerged.

“Why fight?” the bartender said, leaning toward him. “In the end, we all return to the sea which spawned us. You can come willingly and live prosperously with the Esoteric Order. Join us, or...”

Pictures of the last living moments of his wife and daughter swam through Morley’s head; the boat—too small, really, for three people—being tossed on the waves as the black clouds gathered quickly and without warning. Helplessly, he watched the boat being blown across the Sound. The rocking swells washing over the sides of the boat, the screams of his wife, the terrified crying of his daughter were replayed cruelly and with hideous clarity in his mind.

He saw the darkening sky opening up with a deluge of cold, stinging rain as the boat finally capsized leaving him clinging with the bloodied nails of cold, numb fingers while he watched the stricken faces of his wife and daughter sink beneath the ferocious waves. In those last minutes he thought he saw a giant face just beneath the surface of the water, grinning savagely and staring at him through the storm with ancient eyes. And then he saw himself being washed up on the shore. And as these images assaulted his mind, he barely felt the clammy fingers gripping his arms, soaking through the material of his jacket to his skin and lifting him away from the bar.

The unblinking eyes and slack emotionless faces of the pub patrons were forgotten in the traumatic horror of memory.

As he lost consciousness the group hoisted him up and carried him from the pub. His last thought was that the rocking of his body in their spindly arms felt much like bobbing on the waves of the sea.

When he awoke, Morley lay in the wet sand of the beach. He heard the crash of the tide and felt the cold sting of the wind on his exposed face. Beneath the sound of the ocean, he thought he heard voices rising and falling in a frenetic rhythm. He sat up and looked around, disoriented and apprehensive. He was alone on the beach, but far off in the distance he saw the lights of the pub. Shadows capered and swirled behind the yellow-lit windows as if the pub were hosting a ghastly cotillion.

The wind howled across the waves as something huge, dark and dripping raised itself from the water and loomed, black and shining in the limpid moonlight. Morley got to his feet and stared at the creature that swayed above him. He stared into the terribly familiar eyes; eyes he had previously seen beneath him, through the churning waves of the storm-swept ocean as he clung for life to his overturned boat. But where he had felt fear and horror at their first meeting, now he was filled only with an unholy awe.

The chanting voices were growing louder. Morley turned and saw a line of the strange folk emerging from the pub and marching across the beach toward him. Their pale faces were illuminated by flickering lanterns held in webbed fingers. He noticed that, while they were mostly dressed in plain but modern clothes, there were two who wore dark, hooded robes. These two were helped along by the rest, as if walking were difficult for them. As they got closer, Morely saw that one of the robed figures was taller than the group of pallid-skinned, bulging-eyed patrons, and the other much smaller.

Morley grasped the terrible realization before they even threw back their hoods. He moaned and fell to his knees, his vision blurring with tears. The faces were distorted, altered, but still recognizable. He bent over until his face pressed into the sand and cried silently. Hands as cold and damp as the beach caressed him as the chanting grew in volume and intensity. Finally, he raised his head and looked into the piscine eyes before him. Morley rose and took their mucid hands in his, kissing the fingers and marveling at the sensation of soft scales against his lips.

“Wait for me,” he said, embracing the robed figures.

Morley turned and walked toward the sea, feeling the salt-sting against his skin. The chanting behind him swelled with the wind as the looming thing beckoned while slowly sinking into the sea. When the water reached his lips, Morley smiled for the first time in months. Then he disappeared beneath the waves.

Mr. 6 O'clock

"Here he comes."

The three children gathered at the window to watch the old man walk by. Ice-cream-sticky hands clutched at the curtain as they hid themselves from his view. But they needn't have worried; the old man never looked their way. Not today, not any day, not ever. The old man walked with his hatchet-face pointed forward, always.

"Where does he come from?"

"Where is he going?"

The old man walked slowly, but deliberately down the sidewalk, past the houses of the neighborhood. He wore a dark brown suit, brown shoes and a brown bowler hat. His skin was pale and blotched here and there with brown spots. His watery brown eyes seemed never to waver from his path. He walked carefully, but without a cane. The children watched him until he rounded a corner—the same corner every day—and disappeared from view.

In the distance, a church bell finished tolling 6 o'clock.

* * *

"He's weird."

Charles ate the last bite of his chocolate ice-cream bar and wiped his mouth with his sleeve before replying to his younger brother. "You shouldn't say that. You know Mom said we should respect our…our…"

"Elders," said David, the oldest of the three brothers. He was nine. He looked sternly at Peter, the youngest at five. "And Charles is right. He's just an old man, you shouldn't call him weird."

Peter scowled. "But he always walks by at the same time every day. And he always wears the same clothes."

"And have you ever seen him anywhere else?" said Charles, unintentionally siding with the brother he had just chastised. “I mean, around town? At any other time, ever?”

David thought for a moment. “No, but…”

“Weird,” said Peter.

“It’s…strange,” said David. “But there are plenty of folks in town we never see. That doesn’t mean anything.”

“Yeah, but nobody else in town walks by our house every single day at the exact same time wearing the exact same clothes,” said Charles. “And nobody else even knows who he is.”

“We don’t know that,” said David.

“Nobody else has ever seen him,” said Charles. “Even Sherrie Davenport, and she only lives three houses down from us. How come she’s never seen him walk by *her* house?”

“Maybe she has,” said David.

“Uh-uh,” said Charles, shaking his head, “I asked her to watch at 6 o’clock last Tuesday and she said nobody walked by her house. Nobody at all.”

David sat quietly, looking out the window where the old man had been just a few minutes before.

“He looks like a vampire,” said Peter.

"Peter!"

"Well, he does!"

* * *

That night, David lay in bed thinking about the old man in the brown suit. He was probably just someone's grandfather, out for an early evening stroll. The fact that he always passed their house at 6 o'clock wasn't all that strange. It might be a little odd that no one else they knew had ever seen him around town, but there were a lot of people living there and who could know everybody? Besides, some people liked to keep to themselves. The old man probably lived alone and mostly stayed home, watching TV or reading and went for walks in the evening before or after dinner just to get a little exercise and fresh air.

And as for always wearing the same brown suit and hat, well, so what? His own father only owned two suits: a gray and a navy blue. Maybe the old man was poor and could only afford one suit. Or maybe it had some special value to him, like David's Incredible Hulk t-shirt. He'd wear that shirt every day if his mother would let him. Anyway, he thought, drifting off to sleep, he certainly didn't look like a vampire, like Peter had said. No, he just looked like a frail old man. Certainly nothing to be afraid of. Everyone gets old, he thought. It was his last thought before sleep came.

* * *

"See? I told ya!"

Peter was on his knees backwards on the sofa, crouched down and peering through the window. The church bell's ring filled the air. He glanced at the clock on their living room wall: 6 o'clock.

"Every day," said Charles, sitting next to his younger brother, a finger bookmarking where he'd left off reading his Batman comic book. He turned and looked at David across the room. "Well?"

"He's just walking by now," David said into the phone, leaning toward the window to see for himself the old man in the brown suit ambling slowly by. He was silent for a moment, listening, then said, "Are you sure? You were looking?"

Peter and Charles turned away from the window to watch their older brother. David shook his head at them and then said into the phone, "Well, okay. Thanks. See ya." He hung up and walked over to the window. He sat down on the couch with his brothers.

"Sherrie didn't see him?" said Charles.

“No,” David said. “She said she’s been at the window for fifteen minutes, waiting, and didn’t see nobody but Mr. Cosslowe’s dog.”

“Angus,” said Peter, automatically naming the dog as he turned back to the window. The old man was just turning the corner.

“He’s gone,” said Charles, going back to his comic book.

Peter watched the sidewalk for another moment and then turned around on the couch, picking up the remote for the TV and turning on a cartoon.

David went outside to the porch and stood looking first up the street from where the old man had presumably come, and then down the street to where he had disappeared. He stared for a long time at the corner where the old man always turned before finally going back inside.

* * *

Every day at 6 o’clock the old man walked slowly by their house and every day the boys kept watch. It was no longer interesting to them, just a ritual that they had come to accept. The church bell tolled, they went to the window, the old man appeared and shuffled down the sidewalk past their house, never looking right or left, just straight ahead at whatever destination he aimed for. They performed this ritual day after day for a long time, until one day...

* * *

The sound of the distant bell rang through the air and the boys sprang to the window to watch the old man. The bell tolled one...two...three...

"Where is he?" said Peter, craning his neck to see farther down the sidewalk.

Four...five...

"Maybe he's sick," said Charles.

"Maybe he died," said Peter.

"He sure was old," David murmured. "He could've..."

The last reverberation of the sixth bell was followed by silence. The three boys felt something like a hollow sadness inside, although none of them would have been able to articulate it.

Then Peter sat up and pointed. "There he is!"

The old man in the brown suit was indeed walking slowly up the sidewalk, emerging from behind the clump of bushes that served as a fence between their yard and their neighbor's. His brown shoes scraped across the cement, left then right, then left and right again. When he was directly in front of their window, the old man stopped.

The three boys sat silently, unconsciously holding their breath, unable to look at anything but the old man in the brown suit.

Slowly, agonizingly, his head turned on his skinny, fragile-looking neck. It turned until, finally, he was looking directly at the three boys and his watery brown eyes met theirs. He turned and started up the walkway to their house. He reached out a thin, skeletal finger. The doorbell rang.

* * *

The church bell tolled 6 o'clock and the two children peered outside from behind the gauzy curtain.

"It's time," whispered Shane.

"Let me see," said his sister, Dee, stretching on her tiptoes to look past her brother's shoulder at the sidewalk in front of their house.

"Every day," Shane said, as the object of their interest came into view. "Every day at the same time, in the same clothes. Same brown suits, same brown shoes, same brown hats."

“Why?” asked Dee.

“I don’t know,” said Shane, feeling a strange combination of awe and unease.

“It’s weird,” said his sister, pulling the curtain closer so as not to be seen. She need not have worried, though; the passing eyes outside only stared forward, never looking left or right.

Shane nodded, silently agreeing with his sister. It *was* weird. And what was even stranger, whenever he asked his friends or anyone about what they saw every day at 6 o’clock, no one else seemed to know what they were talking about. It was as if the small parade outside was for their eyes only.

When the four identically dressed old men had shuffled past and rounded the corner, the two children inside the house went back to playing video games. But their thoughts constantly strayed to the strange, brown-suited old men, and they would be at the window again the next evening at the same time.

Get Right with God

Nick did another line off the dashboard, then leaned back and savored the explosion inside his brain and the spreading numbness that followed. His darting eyes caught his reflection in the rear-view mirror. He was bathed in the blue light of the neon cross that hung on the church building just across the parking lot. From inside the building came the muffled strains of "Ye Who Are Weary Come Home"; a susurration that hung in the hot stillness of the summer night air. Without realizing it, Nick began to sing along, softly, barely mouthing the words.

When the song ended, Nick reached over and opened the glove compartment, took out a pint of Old Charter, and unscrewed the cap with his teeth while his other hand rummaged inside his jacket pocket. He spit the cap out the driver's side window and took a swig from the bottle while pulling a crumpled pack of smokes from his pocket. Settling back into the seat, Nick lit a cigarette and held it to his lips with a trembling hand. The other hand loosely cradled the bottle of liquor against his crotch. He let the cigarette dangle out the window and watched the smoke drift up into the clear night sky.

Another hymn started—"This World Is Not My Home"—and Nick took another drink and another drag, got out of the car and ambled across the parking lot toward the church building. He took his time, savoring the cigarette and the sound of the gravel crunching beneath his boot heels. He looked up to see the stars and the sky began to spin so he quickly focused on the lighted windows of the church building to keep his bearings.

The Church of Our Redeemer sat on a flat parcel of land just outside of town. Tall, brown grass surrounded the property. Deep in the summer, the grass was full of crickets and tonight they were singing hymns of their own. In front of the building ran Highway 404, which went north to the city and southbound to nowhere.

Behind the church ran the Skalus river, which snaked its way lazily down from the hills and through the county, to eventually empty itself into the sea. The rippling of its waters over mossy stones was a familiar and comforting sound. Along its banks, willow trees were silhouetted against the stars, limbs swaying slightly in a breeze so soft that it did nothing to dispel the heat.

Nick listened to the crickets and river for a while. The singing inside the church had stopped. He walked up to the side of the church building, put his ear to the wall and heard a single, muffled voice, rising and falling. The numbness was wearing off and he felt like a million ants were crawling beneath his skin. He pulled the bottle from his back pocket and took a drink, then wiped his mouth with the sleeve of his denim jacket.

It had been a long time since Nick laid eyes on the church, much less been inside. He remembered helping raise the building when he was a kid. Well, as much as he had been able to, anyway. Mostly he carried two-by-fours around to the men—his father, his uncle and a couple of other fellows from the church. At that time the congregation had been small—mostly family—and they had been holding services in his Aunt Laura's house, with a few metal folding chairs and his Uncle Ewing's drafting table serving as a makeshift pulpit. Uncle Ewing and his father took turns delivering the sermons every other Sunday. But a lot of new people were moving into the area, and several became interested in joining the Church of Our Redeemer. Those new people brought in new people of their own and, before long, Aunt Laura's house was no longer sufficient. The men of the congregation had pulled their resources and bought a patch of land upon which to erect a church building. Nick had fond memories of those days. He remembered being overjoyed the first time he came out to the property with his father and saw that it sat next to the river. It had been summer then, too, and the sound of the crickets and the rushing water seemed eternal.

There were only a few drops left in the bottle and Nick swallowed them with a grimace. He threw the bottle toward the highway and heard the satisfying smash of glass in the darkness. Pushing his sweaty hair back from his forehead, he closed his eyes, inhaling deeply. Then he followed the wall to the front of the church and walked up the steps to the wooden double doors. A dusty yellow porch light barely illuminated the sign that hung next to the doors: Church of Our Redeemer - All Welcome. Services Sun Morn - 10:30 Sun Eve 6:30 Wed 7:30. Nick traced the letters with his fingers. The sign was dusty.

He wiped his fingers on his jeans and grasped the door handle.

The doors swung open, and Nick felt the cool rush of air-conditioned breeze hit his face. He entered the building and stood in the small foyer, looking around. There was a bulletin board with cards, flyers, birthday reminders and various other assorted messages tacked up on it. A drinking fountain was set in the wall to his right. He was suddenly very thirsty. Nick bent over the fountain and turned the handle. An arc of water that smelled of chlorine shot out and Nick drank deeply.

When he finished, he turned to the entranceway that led into the nave. Through the doorway he could see the rows of pews, only about half-full—only the most devout attended evening services—and the pulpit at the other end of the room. The preacher wasn't behind the pulpit, however, but down on the floor in front of the congregation, exhorting them to remember the ultimate sacrifice their Lord had given for their sins.

Nick started walking down the aisle between the pews. As he passed, heads turned. He kept his head pointed straight forward but his eyes darted back and forth, scanning the faces that were watching him. Some gaped in surprise, some looked with mild interest. He recognized several of the surprised faces. There was his cousin, Jamey; he'd stolen Jamey's car—a '69 Charger that he'd spent three years restoring—and driven to Mexico, where he traded it for an ounce of blow, a bottle of tequila and a baggie of peyote buttons.

A couple rows farther and there was the round, wrinkled face of Aunt Pauline, her eyes huge behind the wire rims of her glasses. Aunt Pauline had let Nick crash on her couch the first time he'd gotten out of jail. He lived in her house for a week, eating the meals she made for him, watching Jeopardy with her in the evenings, listening to her read from the Bible at night before they went to bed.

Then one day while Aunt Pauline was at the store buying more groceries, he'd filled his backpack with canned goods from the cupboard, gone through her dresser drawers until he found a roll of bills, which he took without even counting (it turned out to be close to six hundred dollars) and then called an old drinking buddy who came over in his pickup. The two of them then loaded Aunt Pauline's TV set and stereo speakers into the bed of the truck and headed to the nearest pawn shop, then hightailed it to the coast for a while until the money ran out.

He shuffled a little farther down the aisle and saw Mr. Oren, who was glaring at him with a mixture of disgust and anger. Mr. Oren's daughter was Wanda Lee, who Nick had knocked up, promised to marry and then run out on after it was too late to consider any alternative. In the next pew was Larry Corbett, who Nick had once punched so hard he'd knocked out four of Larry's front teeth. Sue Denton, who Nick had spread rumors around town about her having the clap after she clawed and kicked her way out of the backseat of his car one night, beneath the old railroad trestle out on Lantern Lake Road.

There were more familiar faces, none of them especially friendly, but he was almost to the front of the room now and the preacher had stopped his sermonizing and was standing still, back against the pulpit behind him, watching him with wondering eyes.

Nick stopped at the last pew and looked to his right. This was where his mother always sat. The pew was empty now. Nick looked back to the preacher—his father—and marveled at the changes since he'd last seen the man. His skin was sagging, his hair was whiter and thinner, while the glasses he wore seemed thicker. The man's suit was baggy, even though Nick recognized the suit and knew that it had once fit the preacher perfectly.

Something inside him was breaking, something he'd been barely holding together for a long time now. He felt the room spin and he fell to his knees.

"Dad?" he said, reaching out.

The preacher came to him, laid his hands on Nick's head and said, "Son."

"I came to be saved, Dad," Nick said. Then he could no longer hold back the tears and he cried so hard it felt like his ribs were cracking. Between sobs he said, "I'm sorry...so sorry..." His whole body shook. Then his father's arms were around him, guiding him to the front pew. They sat together like that, just holding onto each other, while someone began singing "When the Roll Is Called Up Yonder" and then the whole congregation joined in. Nick and his father whispered together, cried some more, held each other tightly until the song was over. Then his father composed himself, stood up before the gathered flock and gestured toward Nick.

"My son has come to ask for forgiveness." His eyes swept over the congregation. "Forgiveness not only from God...but from his family and his loved ones. He knows he's done wrong. God knows he's done wrong. But God has promised us that if we truly repent then we will be forgiven."

He looked at Nick and nodded. Nick slowly pushed away from the pew and stood awkwardly facing the roomful of people, most of which he had hurt and betrayed at one time or another.

"I know I've made a lot of mistakes," he started, then thought for a moment. "No," he said, "mistakes are made out of ignorance or accidentally. I mostly knew what I was doing. I'm just wicked. I'm a bad person. I've got a rotten soul. But this...this is no way to live. And I don't want to do it anymore. Please," he forced himself to make eye contact with the people he had committed sins against. He expected hostility but was surprised to see...what? Acceptance? Even joy? Yes, he thought most of their faces seemed alight with rapture. Radiant happiness at his return and the confession of his sins. Or was that just self-delusion?

He looked to his father and saw the old man's face. There was no mistaking the look of hope fulfilled, there, like a child who has received exactly the present he wanted for Christmas.

"Do you repent of your sins?" his father asked.

"Yes, I truly do." He looked out at the congregation again. "I'm so sorry...for everything."

"Do you accept Jesus Christ as your Lord and Savior?"

Nick nodded, the cocaine and alcohol in his system being replaced by a euphoria greater than any drug he had ever known. "I do."

"Hallelujah!" his father cried, "Sing His praises!"

The congregation rose up and, as one, began singing "Oh Happy Day" as they gathered around him, smothering him with hugs and voicing their love and forgiveness. Nick tried to imagine what it must be like to be able to do that; to forgive someone as wretched as him and forget about all the damage done. He looked into his own heart and knew that he would never be like these people. He desperately wanted to forgive himself but could not.

Over the noise of song and congratulations, someone shouted out, "To the river!" and he felt his father take his arm and lead him, still surrounded by the flock, out of the church building and into the still, hot night. They headed back behind the church and down the embankment to the rushing water. Nick saw the stars above him in such crystal clarity that he was overwhelmed, and the tears started to flow again. The full moon bathed them in its serene white light.

While the rest of the people remained on the riverbank, his father led him down into the water, both of them still fully clothed, until they were standing waist-deep in the middle of the river. He felt the tug of the current around his body, the shifting rocks and sand beneath his feet. The water was cool and fragrant, and he was glad in his heart.

Now it was quiet but for the chirping of crickets, the rippling water and the slight movement of the drooping willow branches. His father placed his hands on the sides of Nick's face and looked into his eyes.

"Do you want salvation, Son?"

Nick nodded and whispered, "More than anything."

His father addressed those assembled in a loud and steady voice, "Then by the authority granted to me by Our Lord, I baptize you in the name of the Father, the Son and the Holy Ghost."

Nick took a deep breath, savoring the smell and taste of the night air. As his father lowered him toward the water, he let his breath escape slowly. His lungs were empty of air as he was submersed but his eyes remained open. Through the ripples of the water, he could see the wavering face of his father in the moonlight. He gripped his father's hands and willed himself to be like a stone. His body sank to the bottom. Nick saw his father's eyes widen and felt him trying to pull him out of the water, but he was old now and Nick was determined. They thrashed about in the middle of the river. He heard his father yelling and thought he heard splashing to either side of them as people realized what was happening, but he just held onto the old man's hands and calmly opened his mouth. The river rushed into his lungs and the feeling that spread through his body was better than any bump of coke he'd ever snorted, sweeter than any rock he'd ever smoked, more satisfying than any dope he'd ever shot into his veins.

Nick heard singing again; a perfect angelic choir serenading him. The stars above shone strangely clear through the water. For the first time in a long time, he felt at peace. He closed his eyes and let his thoughts drift with the current.

He let the river wash away his sins.

Thirteen Steps

It was getting cold. I pulled my trusty leather jacket tighter around me and checked my phone for the millionth time. Nothing.

The concrete curb was making my ass numb and the wind was picking up. The tree that I sat under showered me with dead leaves. I sent another pissed off text and then took out my switchblade, flicking the blade open and closed just to have something to do. A minute later headlights rounded the curve at the end of my street. I shielded my eyes as they got closer.

Luther pulled up next to me and let his mom's car idle while I took my time getting up, making a big presentation of brushing the dirt off the seat of my pants and adjusting the collar of my jacket. I folded up my blade and stuck it in my boot, pocketed my phone and then got in the car.

Luther sat behind the wheel, checking his phone. The dashboard lights turned his dark skin a sickly green.

"There's twenty-seven messages from you."

"Yeah," I said. "You're late."

"These last ones are really pissy."

I shrugged. Luther grinned. It looked ghastly in the green glow.

"C'mon, let's roll," I said, looking away.

Luther pulled away from the curb and we sped off into the night, scattering leaves in our wake. He cranked the volume on some god-awful hip-hop crap and handed me a pipe. I took a hit and held the smoke in my lungs as I watched the nondescript houses passing by.

God, I hated this fucking town. I'd lived here all seventeen years of my life and couldn't wait to graduate next year and then get the fuck out. As we drove through the neighborhoods, I imagined the people inside those houses: a bunch of robots, plopped down in front of their TVs, laughing when they were told to, getting outraged when they were told to. Drinking shitty beer, eating shitty food. Not living, just existing on automatic pilot. Work, eat, shit, sleep, repeat. Probably the only thing that broke up the monotony was a little violence here and there. Smack the wife around a bit or the kids. Sometimes the other way around. It happened—this was a small town and there weren't many secrets. People talk—it's the only other form of entertainment besides fighting, drinking, and fucking. I laughed at that. I imagined most of those people behind the cracked and peeling facades fucked like they did everything else—mechanical, joyless, passionless, just a function to be accomplished because it was part of the routine, until it wasn't anymore. Maybe they'd had dreams and ambitions once, but now they were beaten down. Stuck here. Stuck in their crappy, nowhere jobs, sick of their spouses, sick of their kids. The kids, like me, hating their parents, hating this town. And we were no better than the rest, really. How many of us were walking around staring at these little devices in our hands, not talking to anyone, lost in our own electronic world? Force-fed the same shit. Consuming it without question.

Most of us.

I slowly let the smoke out in a long sigh and passed the pipe back to Luther.

"Hey, roll the window down, man. This's my mama's car." He hit the pipe, steering with his long legs.

"Change the fucking music, would you, man?" I said, rolling down the window and letting the cold autumn air blow across my face. Luther's mom's car was a 2002 Toyota, and the stereo didn't have Bluetooth, so it was either radio or CDs. Luther reached across me and opened the glove compartment. He rummaged through a bunch of loose CDs—somehow never seeming to take his eyes off the road—and grabbed one that had "Vanessa's 80s Goth" scribbled on it in Sharpie along with a skull inside a heart. I tried to hide a smile. I honestly couldn't tell if Luther liked the same music as us—given a choice he seemed to gravitate toward hip-hop and that cheesy 70s soul shit—but I knew for a fact he liked Vanessa. *Everybody* knew it. Except, apparently, Vanessa.

He ejected the hip-hop cd and slid the new one in. "That better?"

It was Bauhaus. Not my favorite but it would do. Especially for what we had in store tonight.

It was Friday, about 10 pm on a crisp October night, and we were headed for a place called Paradise Valley

Cemetery with the intention of eating some mushrooms, getting good and fried and then testing out a local legend.

It was a weird dynamic, our little group, held together by the tenuous bonds of drugs, music, misplaced admiration, and lust. See, it went like this: Vanessa looked up to Chaney, the wild girl who would do just about anything and didn't give a fuck what anybody thought. Trent was Chaney's current fuckboy, he was good-looking and overconfident, with the muscle but not the brains to back it up. And he had money and easy access to all kinds of drugs, which didn't hurt his position with Chaney, either, and made it easier for the rest of us to tolerate him.

Luther was into Vanessa, which was obvious to just about everyone except Vanessa, herself, as I said. As far as I knew he had never made a move on her, but instead acted as her protector, more like a big brother than a potential boyfriend. Why he didn't go for it, I don't know. Maybe he was worried about what people in our town would think about an interracial relationship. Well, he was probably right to be concerned about that. We didn't exactly live in what you'd call a "progressive" town and Luther was one of only three black kids in our whole school. We all liked to call ourselves "outsiders" and believed we lived on the fringe of society. The difference was, for us suburban white kids that lifestyle was a choice. For Luther...well, it wasn't.

And that leaves me, I guess. What was my story? Well, like Vanessa, I also harbored a grudging respect for Chaney and her "fuck you" attitude. And, like Luther, I also had a hard-on for Vanessa. And like Trent, I liked drugs. So, there you go, three for three. I win. Throw in a mutual liking for punk rock, heavy metal and creepy gothic music and horror movies and you had our little gang.

Anyway, Chaney had found out about this place, Paradise Valley, and about the legend of the 13 Steps to Hell. The story goes that the family who originally built this cemetery were a wealthy Satanic clan and that somewhere in the middle of the cemetery there is a grave where there are thirteen stone steps that lead down into the earth. Apparently, at one time it was the entrance to a lavish underground tomb, long since fallen to ruin, but now the steps just lead to...nowhere.

Except, not exactly.

The legend goes that once you reach the bottom step you will be greeted with a vision of Hell so horrifying that it will drive you insane. That's if you survive. Chaney's cousin, Samantha, was the one who told Chaney about Paradise Valley Cemetery and claimed that she had gone there last year with a group of friends to test out the legend. Pretty much just like we were doing tonight. Samantha said the steps were really hard to find, almost like they existed in another dimension. But they found them, she claimed, and after polishing off a couple bottles of Boone's Farm they Rock, Paper, Scissors'd until the last person standing won the honor of venturing down the steps. Except right as the guy was about to descend, they got hit with spotlights from a couple cop cars parked outside the low walls of the cemetery and they all scattered like rats. Being the bored, drug-addled and unimaginative suburban punks they were, they quickly lost interest in this particular venture and moved on to other things. Probably random acts of vandalism and petty shoplifting. Anyway, they never came back to Paradise Valley.

After hearing this story, I did some research on the internet and found a few accounts of people claiming to have witnessed people going down into the earth only to collapse in terror when they reached the final step, or others who had been driven insane and fled the cemetery. There were even a few disappearances that were blamed on the 13 Steps. One person claimed their friend literally disappeared into the eternal fires of Hell upon setting foot on that thirteenth step.

The cemetery is on privately-owned land, full of family plots. It's surrounded by a lot of fat cat houses so it's not easy to find and a caretaker lives right on the grounds, guarding the place.

"Hey, man, you're gettin' in the back, right?" Luther nudged me, breaking me out of my thoughts, and nodded toward the backseat.

He slowed the car and turned onto a dead-end street. At the end of the street was a cul-de-sac overgrown with blackberry bushes and crooked trees whose branches overhung the houses on the edge of the woods, keeping them in shadow. A broken streetlamp stood rusting away in darkness at the end, slowly being taken over by creeping vines of ivy. There were three houses and each one of them looked haunted. We pulled into the driveway of the middle house. The woods crept so near the house that it looked like a part of nature—a rotten part. There was one light on in an upstairs window. I saw a shapely silhouette in the window for a moment and then the light went out. A few seconds later, the dim, yellow porch light went on and the screen door banged open. Vanessa hopped down the stairs and ran to the car. I crawled into the back seat and let her have shotgun.

"Hey, Luther. Hey, Ricky."

Luther smiled shyly, barely making eye-contact. He fumbled with the zipper on his Raiders jacket while Vanessa settled in, then started backing the car out of the driveway. It would be cute if it didn't turn my stomach.

"Hey, V," I said. She flashed me a devastating smile and then immediately fell in with the music, closing her eyes and slowly rocking her head and body. Her hair was meticulously teased to look like she'd been in bed for a week straight and her eyeliner was also purposefully messy. Nobody took more time and care to appear disheveled than Vanessa.

We headed out of town, the car's speakers pushed to the limit by the dark and heavy rhythm of the music. Luther passed the pipe back to me and I took another hit. I tapped Vanessa on the shoulder and passed it on to her. We continued this triangular ritual until it was cashed. Then I leaned back into the seat and just let the music wash over me. I zoned out and watched as the lights of the passing houses became fewer and fewer and then disappeared as we left the town behind us.

Pretty soon we were on an empty highway with nothing but pine trees on either side of us. I stuck my head out the window and looked up. The branches of the trees grew so close together above the road that it was like we were driving through a tunnel. The air stung my skin and sobered me up a bit. Bauhaus had given way to The Sisters of Mercy and Vanessa sang along. She had a good voice. When I couldn't feel my face anymore, I pulled my head back inside and just spaced out until we started passing lights again.

"I think we're getting close," Luther said.

We were in the suburbs now. The houses here were a higher quality of unremarkable.

"Have either of you heard from Chaney?"

"Not me," I said, not bothering to check my phone. Chaney hadn't sent me a single text since she hooked up with her new boytoy.

"Yeah, I did," Vanessa said, scrolling through texts. "She said they got started late because Trent was still waiting to score the 'shrooms."

"Fuckin' *Trent*," Luther and I said at the said time, both of us rolling our eyes. We caught each other's gaze in the rear view and burst into laughter.

Luther checked his GPS and guided us through neighborhoods that were looking progressively more upscale. I wondered what these people would think if they saw us cruising by; a big, black dude, a goth chick and a sullen, long-haired headbanger, all ripped out of their gourds.

"Where the fuck is this place?" Luther said. "The map says we're there but..."

"Just park, man. Chaney said there's some walking involved." I pulled out the written directions she had given me at school on Monday. "We'll figure it out."

We pulled to the curb in front of a church and Luther killed the motor. We sat in silence, listening to the ticking of the engine, watching leaves blow across the street in the weird orange radiance of the arc-sodium streetlights. I unfolded the paper I'd been given and studied the map Chaney had scrawled.

"Well, this looks pretty simple. It's not far...I think. What street is this?"

"Division," Vanessa said, craning her slender neck to read the sign on the corner.

"Alright, we just head this way," I said, tracing Chaney's pencil trail with my finger. "Looks like we actually have to walk through some people's property to get there."

Luther looked at me and said, "Fuck 'em?"

I nodded. "Fuck 'em."

"Just got a text," Vanessa said, looking at her phone. "Chaney and Trent will meet us there. They're on the way."

"She don't want us to wait?" Luther said.

"Doesn't sound like."

Luther shrugged. "Okay, let's hit it. What do you say?"

"I say let's go get fucked up and party with the devil."

Vanessa laughed and then screeched, "Yeeeeaaahhh!", flashing the devil horns at us with her eyes scrunched up tight so the mascara made them look like empty black slits.

We got out of the car, waited for Luther to lock it up and then headed for Paradise Valley.

Walking through the neighborhoods, I couldn't help thinking about how different my life might be if I had grown up here instead of in town. All the yards were neat and tidy, grass mown to a proper three-and-a-half inches, no broken kid's toys scattered around or rusting cars up on blocks. The houses were bigger, with no plastic covering broken windows or tar paper tacked up to block breezy cracks or holes in the walls. No moss on the roofs. Two and three car garages, most of 'em. Probably with two or three cars actually parked inside, too. But then I thought *bullshit.* The only difference was money.

I bet these people led lives just as pointless and monotonous as any lowlife redneck in our town. I could still see the flickering blue lights of TVs behind the windows. Sure, these TVs were probably flat screen hi-def monsters the size of movie theater screens, but that didn't change what was on 'em. I don't know, maybe some of these people were watching documentaries or something, but I bet most of them were still watching sports or sitcoms or some bullshit "news" like Fox or CNN.

Probably a bunch of functioning alcoholics, too, right? Have a few highballs after a grinding day of pushing those pencils, a little shot in the coffee at breakfast, a couple martinis at lunch. Shit, not only that; if you checked out the medicine cabinets in these houses, you'd probably see rows of pill bottles for any eventuality. Pop an upper in the morning to go with your coffee and toast. A downer at night to go with the highballs and to get you through an evening with the spouse that you still pretend to love in sickness and in health, even though you're banging the chick in the office two doors down or the gardener or pool boy or whoever. The more I thought about it the more I hated these fuckers in their McMansions. I hated 'em more than the poor slobs back in town. At least with those folks you knew where you stood, more or less. I knew that everybody in these neighborhoods were phonies. Rich bitches and slick dicks. Yeah, as we hopped fences and crept through dark backyards the size of football fields I really started to get worked up. I wanted to start putting rocks through those windows. Maybe even break in and bust a few heads. Hold 'em down and pour booze and pills down their throats and then piss on them and every shiny thing they owned. Kill the kids. Rape the wives. Burn it all to the ground and dance in the ashes.

"Ricky!"

Vanessa's whisper cut through my violent thoughts and pulled me back to reality. I was standing right in a bright spot of light on the patio of one of the houses. I could see into the kitchen through a sliding glass door. A fat, balding middle-aged dude in striped boxers stood in front of the fridge with the door wide open, gaping slack-jawed at whatever was inside. All the anger drained out of me at the sight of this poor slob. He didn't look any different than anybody from town, really. Just another sad sack, another cog in the machine. Yeah, his house was massive, and he probably drove this year's model, but I bet he was also in debt up to his ass and he looked like he was on track for a heart attack sometime soon. I doubt he was banging anybody on the side, but you never know. It's a sure bet his wife was cheating on *him*, though. Fuck, I would be if I was her.

"Ricky, come on!"

I stepped out of the light and joined Vanessa and Luther in the shadows as we continued on our way through the neighborhood.

After about ten minutes of trudging through the backyards and side streets, climbing fences, avoiding alarm systems and drooling watch dogs, we came to Paradise Valley Cemetery. It was surrounded by a low rock wall with a few scraggly trees drooping over it here and there. There was a low fog creeping in that was just perfect; made me feel like we were in one of those old black and white Universal monster movies.

"Where's that caretaker's place?" Luther said, scanning the grounds.

"According to this," I said, pointing at Chaney's map, "it's down at the other end. Also, she told me her cousin said the dude's really fuckin' old now and doesn't give a shit anymore."

"Probably just sits in there getting drunk and jerking off," Vanessa said, snickering.

"Nice work if you can get it," I said. They both laughed.

"Should we wait here for Chaney and Trent or head on inside and find this thing?" asked Luther.

I was about to answer when we heard Chaney's voice from somewhere in the darkness behind us.

"Don't even think about ditching us, asshole."

Chaney and Trent materialized out of the fog like ghosts. Chaney looked spectacular, I have to say. Her bright red hair was freshly buzzed on one side and spilling down over her shoulder in a fiery cascade on the other. She wore a leather jacket, too, but newer and not decorated with studs and band patches like mine. Under that was a tight black dress that ended mid-thigh, showing off her ripped fishnet stockings. A pair of oversized motorcycle boots completed her ensemble. Even though Chaney could really grate on my nerves I'd be lying if I didn't admit that she was a stunner. Trent trailed behind her like a puppy. When our eyes met, he straightened up to his full 6' 1" height and adopted a bit of a sneer. I saw through his bullshit, though. He was just a dumb jock that Chaney would use up and discard when she was through with him. But in the meantime, he was an easy drug connection, so I didn't mind putting up with his stupid bravado.

"Hey, girl," Chaney said to Vanessa. Chaney's offhand acknowledgment made Vanessa smile and I was instantly jealous. I hated myself for that.

"Did you get the 'shrooms or what?" I said, anxious to get on with our plan. I was starting to feel agitated. Luther and Vanessa. Chaney and Trent. Our podunk town. This upscale neighborhood. Just fucking everything. All of a sudden, I just wanted to get blazed and see something profound, something *real*. Even if it was Hell, itself.

"I got 'em," Trent said, smirking. He reached into the pocket of his letterman's jacket and produced a Ziplock baggie. "Liberty caps. Enough to fry an elephant's brain."

"Perfect for you," Luther said. He grinned at me. I appreciated the subtle dig at Trent, but my agitation was growing, and I didn't smile back. Of course, Trent didn't get it at all and just continued to smirk at us like we were supposed to drop to our knees and worship him for supplying us with the 'shrooms. Fact is, if I had wanted to put in the effort, I could have scrounged up some liberty caps from any of the surrounding cow pastures back in town. It's just that you have to dig through the cow pies to find them, not to mention dodging the owners of those fields who have been guarding their properties with loaded shotguns ever since the hippies discovered our local psychedelic delights back in the 60s.

"Let's get ripped," Chaney said, grabbing the baggie from Trent. "Come on, you guys, Satan's waitin'." We all gathered around as Chaney passed out the mushrooms, one at a time, in a careful, childlike manner that was almost charming. Then she counted, "One-two-three!" and we all stuffed our handfuls of 'shrooms into our mouths.

Luther grimaced. "Oh my God, these taste like shit!"

He wasn't wrong. I was used to the earthy taste, but this was Luther's first trip and his face continued to writhe until he finally managed to choke down the rubbery mess.

"Alright, let's go find this fucking thing," I said, when everyone was properly dosed. Without waiting for any acknowledgment, I climbed over the rock wall and started walking through the fog toward the center of the graveyard.

I didn't know where I was going but made my way across the cemetery as if I did. Behind me, I heard snickers and giggles, which pissed me off even more. I didn't know why I was so bugged, but I hoped I would mellow out before the 'shrooms kicked in. As I walked, tendrils of fog swirled around my legs like albino snakes. Tombstones glowed in the moonlight. As I passed by them, I let my fingers trail across the cold granite and dig into the damp moss that pervaded the cracks and crevices. For a while I just meandered about, absorbing the atmosphere of the place, and waiting for the 'shrooms to come on. I've spent a lot of time in cemeteries, but this one definitely felt different; older, secretive. I could easily imagine it being haunted or cursed. The more I wandered the more I was losing my bad mood and getting back into the spirit of why we had come.

I must have been walking for at least half an hour, because now I could see statues of angels that seemed to be breathing and shifting their wings as I passed them by. The fog was a phosphorescent green, the color of a moon gone sick. My mouth stretched into an involuntary grin as I looked up and saw multicolored stars swirling around in the sky above me.

Someone bumped into me, hard, bringing me back to reality for a moment.

"Oh, shit, man," Luther whispered. "I think it's happening."

I nodded and heard the bones in my neck grinding together. "Let it ride, man."

"Hey, everybody, over here!"

Chaney's voice echoed through the graveyard and in the thickening fog it was almost impossible to tell where she was. Luther and I meandered our way through what now seemed a maze of headstones until we finally found Chaney, Vanessa, and Trent.

"Check it out," Trent said. Behind them, the lawn of the cemetery sloped down severely, and I saw that it formed a rectangular depression in the earth. I realized we were looking at the spot where the mausoleum had once stood. The walls of the depression still held pieces of stone from its foundation, but they were now overgrown with weeds and what looked like blackberry vines. Strangely, though the fog was still thickening and wrapping around us like a winding sheet, the depression was completely clear, as if the fog refused to penetrate its boundaries.

"Are those the…you know?" Vanessa said. Her voice was barely a whisper but the echoes of it still bounced around inside my head. I glanced at Luther and saw his eyes as big and round as an owl's. Chaney was smiling evilly, her teeth biting her lower lip, and for a second, I thought I saw a thin line of blood trickle down her chin. Trent was giggling and looking up at the fog-shrouded moon. The psilocybin was in full effect now, for sure.

"Guys?" Vanessa said. I had forgotten she had asked a question.

"What?" I said.

Vanessa pointed to the south side of the depression in the earth, and we all looked. Sure enough, a set of stone steps, weather-worn and eroded, descended through the tangle of weeds and vines into the hole.

"Fuckin' A," Chaney said. "Let's check 'em out." She brushed by me, her red hair leaving a trail of fire in the darkness. Vanessa and Trent followed Chaney and I started to, as well, but noticed Luther frozen in place, just staring into the pit with those owl eyes.

"Hey, buddy, how ya doin'?"

No response. I reached out to touch him, my arm seeming to stretch like rubber. It might have been a second or an hour, but my fingers finally connected with the material of his jacket. I pushed carefully, not sure how much strength I was using; I didn't want to send him tumbling into the hole.

Luther jumped at the contact and turned those big owl eyes on me, his pupils so dilated they felt like black holes that I would fall into if I wasn't careful.

"What?" he said. "What?"

"You okay, man?"

Luther shook his head. "This shit is intense, bro."

I couldn't argue with that. Instead, I just indicated with a nod of my head that we should follow the rest of the crew over to the steps.

"Who's going first?" Vanessa said once we had joined them. Trent giggled again and Chaney punched him in the arm.

"Trent will," she said. Her hair was still a halo of fire. Her eyes glowed green and the dark red of her lipstick made her grinning mouth seem like a bloody gash.

We all gathered at the top of the steps and looked down. Sure enough, I counted thirteen of them, leading down into the earth; into the pit that was strangely devoid of fog.

"Who, me?" Trent said.

"Yeah, you, laughing boy," Chaney said, giving Trent a shove toward the steps.

"Fuck, hold on, hold on," he said, pinwheeling his arms before his foot could touch the first step, which was sunken slightly below the ground where we stood.

"Come on," Chaney said, "this is what we're here for. Let's get it on, dude."

Trent, not giggling anymore, rubbed his hands over his face a few times as if that might help sober him up. Then he took a deep breath, looked at us, then looked down the steps into the darkness below.

"Alright," he said, raising his foot slowly. It seemed like hours before the sole of his shoe touched the first decaying step. When he didn't burst into flame or get engulfed by a demon's wings, he stood a little straighter and took a second step. He looked over his shoulder at us and smiled. I expected him to start giggling again but he didn't. Instead, he turned back around and took another step. Three. Four. Five.

On the sixth step, he stopped.

I think we were all holding our breath, waiting to see if he would continue or turn around. I hadn't expected to really be freaked out by this little escapade; it was just something to do. Something to avoid the crushing boredom of another Friday night in Nowheresville. But as I watched Trent lift a trembling foot, I felt real fear shoot through me. Even Chaney had stopped smiling; that bloody gash on her face was now just a wilted rosebud. Luther's owl eyes were transfixed, and his jaw was slack. His tongue squirmed inside his mouth like a bloated worm. Vanessa's pallid face was that of an antique porcelain doll's, her eyes just black empty sockets. It took me a moment to realize her eyes were closed and all that runny mascara was being transformed by the drugs in my system, that her face wasn't really a dilapidated doll skull.

"Do it, fucker!" Chaney suddenly screamed. She was trying to sound tough, pissed off, but I heard the tremor in her voice that betrayed her fear.

I turned my attention back to Trent. His foot touched the seventh step and his body jerked like he'd been struck by lightning. He stood there shaking for I don't know how long—time on 'shrooms is deceptive—then turned and ran back up the steps. He tripped on the top one and fell flat on his face in the grass.

That broke the spell.

Chaney was the first to burst out laughing. Then Vanessa joined in. Finally, even Luther, who really didn't seem to be enjoying his trip at all, started to chuckle.

I was the only one who didn't laugh.

Trent pushed himself up off the grass and stood, panting. His eyes were wild and twitchy. He was still shaking.

"Holy fuck did you guys see that shit?"

"All I saw was a chicken-shit do a faceplant," Chaney said, still laughing.

Trent looked from one face to the next. I guess because I was the only one not laughing, he zeroed in on me. He stumbled forward and fell to his knees in front of me. I tried to back up, but he grabbed my jacket with desperate hands, halting my retreat.

"You saw it?" he said, yanking on my jacket. "Right? Tell me, man."

I shook my head. "I didn't see shit, man."

Trent looked like he was about to say something else, then he just let go of my jacket and slumped forward, his face in his hands. "Oh, fuck. Oh, shit. It was Hell, dude, I was in Hell, I swear to God. Fucking flames everywhere...like, dead people coming up the steps. Their fucking skin was dripping off, man. Oh, God. Oh, fuck."

"It's the 'shrooms, you idiot," Chaney said, still laughing. "You're tripping balls."

Trent raised his eyes, looking from me to Chaney. "You think?" he said. "It seemed so real."

"What else did you see?" Luther asked. He sounded scared.

"Never mind," Chaney said. "That shit sounds wild, and I don't want it ruined for me. I'm going next."

"No," I said, "I am."

I wasn't sure why I said it. I hadn't planned it, it just slipped out.

"The fuck you are," Chaney said, heading for the steps. I quickly moved in front of her, blocking her way.

"I said I'm going next."

She started to say something but then stopped, looking at me strangely. Then she held up her hands and took a couple steps back. "Whatever, dude. You don't gotta be a dick about it."

I looked around at our group; Chaney in her leather jacket and fishnets, half-shaved head and cascade of unnaturally red hair; Luther, blending in with the dark so that the glowing orbs of his wide, staring eyes were almost all I could see of him; Vanessa with her teased hair and runny makeup and trashy black clothes—our thrift-store Madonna; and Trent, one of the popular crowd, a jock slumming it with the weirdos for as long as Chaney would keep him around. The fog swirled around them, obscuring them. When all I saw was a wall of glowing white, I turned and started down the steps.

One, two, three...I counted as I slowly descended. On step six I stopped. The next one was where Trent lost his shit and I wanted to be ready. I heard voices above me but I didn't look back. I lifted my foot and lowered myself down...

Seven.

Suddenly, the air seemed to thicken around me. I was moving in slow motion. When I looked up at the sky, I saw nothing, no stars, no moon, no fog. Just blackness. I couldn't hear their voices anymore. I couldn't hear anything, no crickets, no wind in the trees. Nothing.

Eight. Nine. Ten.

I stopped again. The air seemed to lighten up again. Below me, I no longer saw the overgrown grass and tangles of blackberry vines. Just a softly glowing light.

Eleven. Twelve.

I stopped with one foot hovering over the last step. The light in front of me was growing, spreading. There were pictures in the light. Figures.

What the hell.

Thirteen.

I was standing in the living room of a house. It was a nice house. Very middle-class. Very suburban. Someone was sitting on a couch, watching TV. Some bland-looking dude in his thirties, blue dress shirt undone at the collar, his tie laying across the arm of the couch. Beige Dockers. Expensive haircut. He was drinking a beer—a bottle of some local microbrew. Then a woman appeared from the kitchen. She stood in the doorway, hands nervously wringing a towel. Her hair was neatly done, and she was wearing a modest, nondescript, knee-length dress.

"Bill, dinner might be a little late tonight. I had some trouble with the carrots. The glaze…it didn't really turn out the way it was supposed to." Her voice was tremulous, but familiar.

The dude—Bill—set down his beer and leaned forward, rubbing his temples with his hands.

"You followed my mom's recipe, didn't you?"

“Y-yes,” the woman said. Man, that voice…

“And you fucked it up?”

“No, I…it’s just that it didn’t—”

“I work all day and all I ask for is a decent dinner. *On time*.”

“Yes, it’s just that—”

Bill moved quickly. He grabbed the beer bottle and threw it at the woman. It shattered right near her head. She screamed, ducked and then started to cry. Her mascara began to run.

Oh fuck. Oh no.

It was Vanessa.

Or some version of Vanessa. Vanessa as she would be in about ten years.

Bill came up off the couch and was on her in an instant. His right hand went up and down three times. I heard the sickening sound of meat slapping against meat. I tried to move but I couldn’t. All I could do was watch. I felt my fists clenching and my eyes began to burn.

Bill went back to the couch and started changing channels with the remote. Vanessa was curled into a whimpering ball in the doorway.

“Fix those fucking carrots,” Bill said. Then added, almost pleasantly, “And, hey, get me another beer, would ya?”

Blackness again.

When the light came back, I was standing in an office. Not anything fancy. Just some mid-level, boring-ass office. Looking around, I couldn’t even tell what the fuck they did here. Just some cubicles and a few of those posters on the wall that are supposed to motivate you or something; a kitten dangling from a rope with the words “Hang In There” written across the bottom. Shit like that. There were a few mousey-looking men and women sitting in front of computers. Bags under their eyes. Dandruff flakes on their shoulders. Bellies going to pot. Cheeks sagging in the beginning of what would become jowls. A door opened across the room and a woman came in pushing a cart with stacks of what looked like bundles of printer paper. This time I knew right away. The hair was close-cropped—almost a buzz-cut—but still fiery red. Her eyes were lifeless and her lips—very light pink, not blood red—were turned down in a slight frown. She wore a gray suit jacket, white blouse and a navy-blue skirt. Sensible shoes. I think that’s what got me most, sensible fucking shoes.

“Hey, that report done yet?” a voice bellowed. A door was open on the other side of the room and a rumpled walrus with an obvious comb-over was leaning out, glaring at Chaney.

“No, sir,” she said. I couldn’t believe how tame, how *beaten-down*, she sounded. “I’ve been—”

“I don’t give a good goddamn what you’ve been,” the walrus shouted. The computer-zombies steadfastly kept their eyes on their screens, but I saw a couple of them jump at the sound of his bellowing. “I need that report and I need it *today*; do you understand me?”

“Yes, sir,” Chaney said. Her eyes were downcast the entire time.

“Good. Now get to it.” The door slammed. Before the darkness took me again, I saw the slump of Chaney’s shoulders as she left the cart of printer paper where it stood and took her place in her cubicle amongst the rest of them.

I heard that sickening meat-slapping sound again before the darkness lifted once more. Gradually, a gray light faintly illuminated three figures standing over a fourth. We were in a basement or a small warehouse, maybe—it was hard to tell. It didn’t matter. What mattered was that one of the standing figures was obviously Trent and the huddled figure on the floor was Luther. His shirt was torn, and his face was bruised and bleeding. One eye was dangerously swollen. I saw two teeth lying on the floor next to him. Trent was sweating. His hair—a little longer than it was now—hung across his forehead in wet clumps. He was breathing hard. The other two men hovering over Luther were cookie-cutter replicas of Trent. Good-looking, in-shape, jock types. They had smug, amused looks on their faces.

"I fuckin' told you, man," Trent said, giving Luther a vicious kick in the ribs. Luther, already on his knees, groaned and doubled over, then fell sideways to the floor. The other two guys laughed, and Luther began to spit blood. "I told you to keep your goddamn hands off her. But did you listen—no!" He punctuated the "no" with another kick, this time to the head. Luther didn't groan anymore. I was pretty sure he was out cold.

One of the other guys hocked a loogie onto Luther and his buddy laughed again.

"Man, this motherfucker," Trent said, walking in a circle around Luther's prone body like a wolf admiring its kill. "Nobody even wants his kind around here, much less messin' around with our women." He leveled another kick into Luther's meaty thigh. He didn't move at all; he just lay there in a growing pool of blood. "You brought this on yourself, man. This is what you fuckin' deserve, do you hear me?" Spittle flew from Trent's lips as he leaned down to shout at the unconscious man lying broken and bloodied on the concrete floor.

The other two guys laughed and high-fived each other like they'd just scored the winning run.

I felt like I was going to puke.

Darkness took me again.

Then a dim, gray light. Another apartment. A ratty-ass, one-bedroom hovel. I saw the profile of a man sitting in a worn recliner; emaciated, balding. He was staring at a TV, watching a rerun of some old 1960s sitcom. Not laughing. Not even smiling. He clutched a can of Pabst Blue Ribbon, and his yellowing t-shirt was stained with what looked like spaghetti sauce. There were no pictures on the walls of his apartment. No sign of any family or friends. I walked over to the one window in the place and looked outside. Below me I saw a grimy alley filled with overflowing trash cans. A guy was huddled up against one of them, frantically trying to shove a needle into his arm with a shaking hand.

There was a touch on my shoulder, and I turned around to see the man standing before me. Now that I was facing him, I saw that half his head was missing. Pieces of brain and fragments of his broken skull slid down his neck. Those stains weren't spaghetti sauce, after all. His one eye stared at me, imploringly. Something passed between us. When he was sure I understood, he smiled a rictus smile, went back, and turned off the TV and then laid down on the floor, his foot accidentally kicking the shotgun that I hadn't seen before lying on the other side of his chair. He crossed his hands over his chest. I saw that bony chest rise once and then he was still.

The next thing I knew, I was standing at the top of the steps, feeling the cool night air on my face. I looked up and saw the moon and stars again. Out of the gently swirling fog, faces and figures formed.

"Well?" Chaney said. "What did you see?"

"Ricky, it looked like you...disappeared," Vanessa said.

"Bullshit," Chaney said. But she didn't sound so sure of herself.

"Did you see it? Was it...was it Hell?" Trent whispered.

I looked around at all my friends again. I thought about who they were...who *we* were. We thought we were rebels. Outlaws. Punks. Society's proud outcasts. Truth is, what we really were, was full of shit.

A song started running through my head, *No future. No future. No future for you.*

"Yeah," I said. "Yeah, I saw it. You were right, Trent. It really was Hell."

I reached into my jacket pocket and brought out my switchblade. What I had seen didn't have to be our fate. There was still a chance. Live fast, die young. And leave a good-looking corpse.

My thumb touched the button and, for just a second, I admired the moonlight on the blade before I went about my work.

It wasn't too late.

I would bring salvation to us all.

Winter of the Witch

I. THE COMING OF THE SNOW

Winter was uncommonly cruel that year. The first snow came early—before Thanksgiving—and brought a smile to everyone's face, except Grandpa Jake, who looked like he'd been betrayed by his best friend when he saw the woods covered in glistening white. When I asked him why, he just said he had a feelin'.

Sallie and me were especially glad. Pa let us off our chores early so we could play around in it. Sallie built snowmen and made snow angels and I trudged the two miles over to Billy Ray's so we could have a snowball fight. I might have made a few snow angels, myself, on the way home when nobody was looking. Billy Ray and his family left for the city a few weeks later, to visit relatives, and stayed through Christmas and well into the new year. That made the holidays a little more lonesome than usual as they were our closet—our *only*—neighbors for miles around. Turns out it was probably just as well that they was gone.

Pa still wasn't working, due to getting himself hurt on the skidder, but he and Mama assured us we had a good amount saved up and that he'd be back on the logging crew next spring.

That snow was melted and gone by December, and everything was back to normal for a couple of weeks. But come Christmastime the temperature was dropping pretty steady day by day. Every morning was a hard frost that never melted, just got thicker and thicker. The pond was froze over so thick and fast I saw a bullfrog captured in mid-swim. His back legs was kicked out and his eyes were open and bulging. A couple days after I spied him, the pond had thickened up so much that he was just a smudge of dark green in an ever-widening stretch of blue-white ice.

Then the snow came back, this time to stay.

Now it was Grandpa Jake who was the only one grinning after about two weeks of constant freezing weather, bitter winds and even more snow. But he wasn't grinning out of gladness; it was more like the grin I saw on Davey Lasher's face right before he jumped off Wilder Creek bridge because Tom McKenzie and Frank Terrell wouldn't quit calling him 'sissy' until he did it. Davey broke both his legs and an arm and hasn't ever been right in the head again since that.

Pa and Grandpa Jake were out in the barn with the animals a lot, trying to keep them warm. The cows didn't want to give milk and were behaving very sluggish. A few chickens froze to death. The rest of the hens were like the cows; them eggs was few and hard to come by. We were running low on food and supplies. Pa was able to make it into town just once before the road became impassable. He tried one more time but the crank on the Model T was froze solid, so it didn't matter anyway. Then he saddled up Delilah and tried to ride her into town, but it like to killed her; that mare was too old for that much work in such mean weather. That was the last time we was able to get any kind of groceries. Mama had put up some cans last season but not as much as usual on account of Baby Lynn being born around the time, she usually made her preserves. So, we had food for a while, but it was getting mighty scarce. Seemed like every evening the supper on our plates was getting smaller and smaller.

Winter just kept on keepin' on. The snow and ice seemed like they was never going to quit. We lost two cows and five more chickens. The cat went missing. Pa even let our dog, Charlie, stay inside with us. He'd lay in front of the fire and whine in his sleep. After a while, though, that fire also became a source of worry. The wood Pa and me had put up that summer was fast disappearing. Grandpa Jake said he'd never seen such a bastard of a winter in all his years. I'm sorry to cuss, but that's what he said. He didn't say it around Mama, though, you can believe that.

We muddled along for a while, but it was apparent we'd got to get into town some way or other. One morning in early February, Pa decided he was going to have to walk, said there just wasn't no other way. Mama and Sallie begged him not to, but Grandpa Jake gently took them aside as Pa bundled up in just about every piece of clothing he had. I made up a pot of coffee and filled a thermos with it, then filled another with water and gave them both to Pa. Granda Jake draped a rucksack over Pa's shoulder and fixed a pack on his back so he could bring back as much food as possible. The last thing Pa did was take Mama aside for a private goodbye, then he slung his rifle over his shoulder, and it was time to go. Grandpa Jake and I walked with Pa through the nearly waist-high snow for about a quarter of a mile while Mama and Sallie kept Charlie in the house so's he wouldn't chase after Pa. Just that bit of a walk gave me a sour feeling about Pa's chances of making the 20 miles to town and back.

"Now, Joe, I want you to know if anything happens to me you got to be the head of this family, alright?" Pa said to me as we were about to part. "That means I'm going to have to ask you to grow up maybe a little faster than you wanted to. You're goin' to have be responsible and you'll have to be able to make some tough decisions."

"What about Grandpa Jake?" I asked.

"Grandpa Jake's a good man, but his best years are behind him." He shook his head. "Nope, you're the man of the house now, Joseph. I want you to take care of your ma and sisters. Protect them. At any cost."

The way he was talking scared me. "But you'll be back," I said. I could feel the tears trying to push their way out of my eyes, but I wouldn't let 'em. They would have like to froze right on my face if I did. That's what I told myself, anyway.

"That's right," Pa said, smiling down at me. "But just in case, alright? We've got to be prepared. Can you do that for me, son?"

I nodded and said "yessir," and Pa nodded back. Then he and Grandpa Jake shook hands and Pa said something into Grandpa Jake's ear that I couldn't hear. Then he turned and began slogging through the snow.

That night the wind howled fiercely, and more snow fell. I sat at the stove and kept the fire going, being thrifty with the wood. I knew Pa was strong. He was probably the toughest old bull around these parts, even with his injury. But he was only a man. And this night weren't fit for man nor beast.

About midnight Grandpa Jake came out and told me to go on to bed, he'd tend the fire. Said he couldn't sleep for having Pa on his mind, anyway. Well, I could have told him the same, but I knew he was doing me a charity, so I didn't argue. We sat together a while by the fire, each of us thinking our own thoughts, yet probably thinking about the same thing. Grandpa Jake got out his pipe for a smoke just as I was fixin' to go on to bed. He grunted as he undid his tobacco pouch. "That's the last of it," he said, frowning, packing the pipe. I paused a moment longer to admire it. It was beautifully carved out of bone—Pa said it was some kind of whale bone—with curious creatures dancing along the bowl and some words carefully etched on the stem in a language I didn't understand. Pa once told me it was Tlingit, and that Grandpa Jake got it from that Indian clan way up north in a place called Alaska when he was young. I'd never had an inclination to take up smoking—not yet anyway—but I admired that pipe, just the same. I kissed Grandpa Jake on his scruffy cheek, said my goodnights and slipped off to my room.

I wondered if anybody was sleeping tonight. Even Baby Lynn, normally quiet through the nights (a rare blessing, Mama always said), I could hear was making upset noises. I looked in on Sallie and saw her bed was empty, so I quietly cracked upon the door to Mama's bedroom and saw her and Sallie and little Baby Lynn all piled up together, cozy-like. I closed the door and went on to my room, feeling kind of lonely and anxious. I felt too worried to sleep. So, I just sat on the corner of my bed for a while, looking out my window at the whirling snow. It was kind of peaceful, watching the flakes falling and twirling around in the wind, and I started to feel calmer and sleepy, after all. I crawled under the covers but immediately began chastising myself for finding beauty in something that was no doubt causing my father all kinds of hardships, knowing he was alone out there, somewhere. But I fell asleep before I could get too far with that line of thinking.

The next morning, I woke up to a blue sky and the sun shining through the window. It was a small relief to see that the snow had stopped, but it was still bitter cold, so I knew that it wasn't going to make much difference at this point. Not for Pa, at least. I got out of bed, wrapping a blanket around me, and went to check the fire. Grandpa Jake was sitting slumped over the kitchen table, fully dressed. At first, I thought he was asleep, and I wondered had he been there all night or just got up ungodly early. But when I came near the stove he sat up and said, "Just put a log on 'bout half an hour ago." I nodded and he said, "Sure could use some coffee, though."

As I ground the beans—which were getting worrisome scarce—and boiled the water, I started to pray. Praying wasn't something I—or any of us, except Mama—did very often. It was awkward trying to find the right words, but I counted on God knowing what was in my heart. That's what Mama always said, "God knows what's in your heart." I hadn't had much use for God until now, but I was so worried about Pa that I was willing to give it a try. I didn't know how much God was going to count my previous lack of interest against me, though.

When the coffee was ready, I ended my prayer for my father's safe return with an "in Jesus' name, amen", then poured two steaming cups and carried them to the table. Grandpa Jake picked up his cup and held it under his nose, feeling the heat in his hands and letting the smell wake him up a little.

"Your mama and sister'll be up soon," he said, his throat all froggy with morning. "I think I'm going to go out and check the traps, you wanna come. Breakfast'll probably be ready for us by the time we get back."

I couldn't see much point in checking the traps. He and Pa had set out those traps almost a month ago and they'd stayed empty this whole time. I figured any creature with sense that was worth eating was probably holed up somewhere, waiting out this merciless winter. But, then again, what else could we do? At least we'd feel like we were trying something. And who knows, maybe we'd got lucky this time and snagged a rabbit or a squirrel or something.

"We'll take our rifles, too," Grandpa Jake said, getting up from the table with a cracking and popping of his old bones. "Head down by the lake and see if we can scare up some grouse."

I nodded and drank down my weak coffee. Something in his eye told me that the traps and the grouse was just an excuse to get us out of the house for a while, but I didn't know why.

I heard Mama's bed creak and a couple minutes later she was standing in the kitchen doorway, yawning and rubbing her neck with one hand and holding a still sleeping Baby Lynn in the other. Her beautiful golden hair hung down her back. I hadn't seen it that way for a while and it was a little shocking how much gray was now mixed in there with the yellow.

"What are you two doing up so early?" she said, digging around in the pantry. I knew she was on the scrounge, trying to conserve food like I was conserving the firewood. I got up and poured her a cup of coffee and mixed in some cream and sugar, even though we was also getting mighty low on those. Mama was the only one who took it that way; Pa, Grandpa Jake and me all took ours black.

"Going out to check the traps," Grandpa Jake said, getting on his boots. He glanced over at me and said, "Go get yourself dressed, boy."

"Yes, sir," I said, pouring myself another cup. I took it with me to my room and sipped on it while I put on my thickest wool socks, two shirts and a sweater. Then I laced up my boots and took my cup back down the hall with me. Before I got to the kitchen I checked in on Sallie, cracking Mama's door a little bit and peeking inside. She was still sleeping, a lump underneath a pile of blankets. I closed the door and went to the kitchen, washed my cup and set it on the towel next to the sink. Mama was already mixing up batter for pancakes and had laid out a few measly strips of bacon. There were worry lines on her forehead that hadn't been there a few weeks ago and her eyes had a faraway look in them.

"Let's go, boy."

Grandpa Jake was standing by the door, all bundled up with his Remington cradled in his arms. I gave him a nod and got my coat off the hook, slipped it on and pulled my hat down over my ears. I pulled on my gloves and then went and got my Winchester down from the rack.

"Ready," I said.

Grandpa Jake nodded. He went over and kissed Mama on the cheek and said we'd be back in an hour or so. She nodded and tried to smile. Her eyes looked like she'd been crying, but there were no tears on her face.

"You two be careful out there," she said.

"We will," I said. I gave her a little kiss, too, and then called Charlie. He'd been sleeping by the stove, but he jumped up immediately when I said his name. But Grandpa Jake put a heavy hand on my shoulder and shook his head.

"Leave the dog," he said.

Charlie whined a bit as we went out the back door without him. Now I was really curious about what Grandpa Jake had in mind. We always took Charlie with us whenever we went out hunting. He was old but still spry and he took these things personally.

We walked through the backyard and into the woods. The snow wasn't as deep here due to the tree cover and walking was a bit less tricky and toilsome. I waited for Grandpa Jake to say something, but he just stared ahead and kept up a middling pace. So, we hiked through the woods in silence, which gave me the opportunity to gaze at our surroundings. Once again, despite my concerns over Pa's journey, I was struck by the beauty of it all; that untouched virgin white blanket that lay silent over everything and sparkled here and there where patches of sun cut through the trees. Our breath streamed out behind us as we walked, and it didn't take long before I couldn't feel my face. Under the trees we didn't feel the wind as much, but it was still there; it moaned through the tops of the pines and once in a while would knock off a clot of snow that had built up in the boughs. But there was no birdsong and no sounds of any other living thing, except for our breathing and the crunch of our boots in the snow, and the woods started to seem oppressive in a way they never had before. We walked like that for quite a ways. Normally, it took about a quarter of an hour to walk to the lake, but I knew with all this snow it would be a lot longer.

"Look here."

I pulled up before walking straight into Grandpa Jake's backside; I'd been thinking about Pa again and not watching where I was going. Grandpa Jake was standing spread-legged and pointing down at the ground. I looked where he aimed his finger and saw two sets of tracks in the snow. They led out of the woods to the north and continued on into the trees to the south, but directly in front of Grandpa Jake the snow had been thrashed about as if there had been some kind of ruckus or like a madman had danced a jig there for a while. There were two kinds of tracks; one looked like a dog or a wolf, but much bigger than any I'd ever seen before. Bigger than I ever imagined they *could* be. The other tracks were human, small like a woman, and barefoot. But who would be crazy enough to be walking around in the snow without any boots on? The tracks went side by side up to the spot where we stood and then they mixed together. I rubbed my eyes with my gloved hands and tried to swallow down the lump of fear that had just formed in my throat.

"What are they?" I asked Grandpa Jake. My voice came out in a whisper even though I hadn't intended it to.

He looked at me, then looked up at the sky, then squatted down and put his gloved hand over one of the wolf-like tracks. Even with his fingers all splayed out, his hand couldn't cover the whole thing.

"I heard 'em last night." Grandpa Jake said, his face grave. His eyes were hard little black beads glaring out from underneath the brim of his hat.

"Heard who?" I asked. I was starting to be afraid, although I didn't know the reason why. But I felt a darkness trying to creep over me that I didn't welcome, and it made me want to run. I told myself I was being a jackass, but it didn't relieve the feeling any.

Grandpa Jake stood up slowly, and in the silent woods the cracking of his old joints seemed loud as gunshots. He was shaking his head slowly and his eyes were shifting back and forth, trying to take in the whole forest, it seemed. He put his hand on my shoulder, and I felt it trembling. I told myself it was because of the cold and that he was just feeling his age, but deep down I knew that he was covered in that same creeping darkness that was troubling me.

"Let's get back," he said, turning around. "We'll have ourselves a little talk."

"What about the traps?"

"Forget 'em," he said, not looking back. "It's too late. If there was any game to be had around here our traps ain't what's gonna get 'em."

We walked back to the house, this time with me looking over my shoulder every few seconds. Grandpa Jake just trucked along, staring straight ahead. If the walk was any strain on him, he didn't show it.

We got back to the house and kicked the snow off our boots on the back porch. Grandpa Jake grabbed my elbow before I could open the door and gave me a look. He didn't say nothing, but I knew well enough what he was telling me: don't mention those tracks to Mama or Sallie. I gave him a quick nod and then we went inside.

Mama had breakfast laid out on the table. Sallie was slowly eating her pancake, cutting off one little bite, swirling it around in the little bit of syrup and butter Mama was able to spare, then poking it into her mouth and chewing it like our cows used to chew their cud. Then she washed it down with a sip of watery-looking milk. Baby Lynn sat at the end of the table in her highchair, with a bowl of mush in front of her that looked untouched. Mama was still at the stove, frying bacon. She turned when she heard the door close. She had put up her hair, but one long strand had escaped and hung down in her face. I went to her and tucked it behind her ear.

"We're back, Mama."

She smiled at me; a tired sort of smile that didn't reach her eyes. "That was quicker than I expected. Any luck?" she said.

I just shook my head. Grandpa Jake came up behind me and clapped me on the shoulder. "Let's get out of these wet clothes and get us some breakfast," he said. He gave Mama a wink. "Smells heavenly, Sarah."

Mama and Grandpa Jake's eyes met, and something passed between them. Some grownup thing I didn't yet understand. I suspected it had to do with Pa, some unspoken understanding. I went back over to the back door and shrugged off my coat, hung it, along with my hat, on the hook there, then took off my boots and walked to the table in my stocking feet. My socks were wet, so I peeled those off and reached over to the stove, laying them next to Charlie. He hadn't even bothered to get up when we came in, so I figured he was still offended that he'd been left behind.

After breakfast, Mama laid Baby Lynn down and took Sallie into the back room for her daily lessons. Grandpa Jake and me sat back down at the table. He took out his pipe and fiddled with it, tapped it lightly on the table a couple of times. That was about all he could do with it since he'd run out of tobacco the night before. I figured he just liked the feel of it in his hands.

After a few minutes of us listening to the fire crackling, Grandpa Jake leaned forward and cleared his throat. His eyes roamed the room, looking everywhere but at me and I noticed a tremble in his voice when he finally spoke.

"I don't b'lieve your daddy'll be comin' back," he said. He barely spoke above a whisper, but his words still felt like a punch to my heart. "Them tracks out there...bet you've never seen the like."

"No sir," I said, trying to keep the quiver out of my voice.

"No," he said, shaking his head, "I don't reckon you would have." He slowly twirled the pipe around in his gnarled old fingers, thinking on what to say next. Finally, he said, "They ain't never been in these parts. Not this far south. Not to my knowledge, at least. Then again, I ain't no expert and wouldn't want to be. Those that is, their souls must be damned."

I didn't know what any of this meant and I didn't like the way his black eyes kept darting around the room, like he was expecting something to bust through the door any second. I was ignoring the part about him saying my Pa wasn't going to make it back, because that had already been in the back of my mind, anyway. I suddenly felt a coldness caused by something other than this merciless winter creeping over me.

"Them tracks," Grandpa Jake said, leaning in even closer, "I fear they was made by a *waheela* at the beck and call of a *naak'w s'aati*".

The words made no sense to me and for a moment I worried that my grandfather had suddenly gone senile. I waited for Grandpa Jake to explain but he was grimly staring down at the pipe gripped in his leathery hands.

There was a low, mournful sound outside that might have been the wind howling, but I wasn't sure.

"I don't understand, Grandpa," I said, when I couldn't stand his silence any longer.

Grandpa Jake finally looked up at me with watery eyes, rimmed with red. "She's found me, boy," he said, his voice a raspy whisper. "She's found me at last after all these years."

The moaning sound outside was growing louder. I got up from the table and went to the window. With my shirtsleeve I wiped a spot on the frost-covered glass and peered outside. The sky had clouded up again, a gray shroud over the sun. The day had gone dark. The snow no longer sparkled but was now just a flat, dead white.

"Why did you say that about Pa?" I asked. My breath fogged up the spot on the window I'd just cleared.

"Come back over here, boy," Grandpa Jake said. "I've got something to tell you."

II. GRANDPA JAKE'S STORY

I turned away from the window, even as I thought I saw a dark form, blurred by frost, drift out of the forest. But when I looked back it was gone, so I walked slowly over to the table and sat down across from Grandpa Jake. His hands still fiddled with the pipe, turning it over and over, running his fingers across the carvings. When he spoke, his voice was the old Grandpa Jake I was used to, firm and steady, but he seemed unwilling, or unable, to meet my gaze. Instead, he kept his eyes lowered to the table and that strangely carved pipe.

"I want you to know this is a true story, though it may sound like a tall tale or one of those fairy stories your mother used to read to you at bedtime. Except no story in any of them books could ever be as terrible, as ghastly, as what really happened.

"My folks ran a mercantile in White Horse when I was a boy. My pa was a hard man, but decent, until my ma died of the pox. Then he took to the bottle and by and by got a little too handy with the belt. So as soon as I was old enough to do for myself, I took off. I was trying to earn my living as a miner up in the Yukon territory. Luck in that particular profession eluded me, though. Twenty years hence the Klondike would be overrun by men with gold fever when a big strike was discovered there, but I was long gone from the territory by then. But at that time, I was a young man, and hearty. Every day was an adventure in that wild land and that's what I craved back then, adventure.

"My wanderings took me across the Yukon to the coast of Alaska. I eventually gave up on mining and would take odd jobs here and there as I traveled. It was in Chilkoot that I got a job working at the livery stable, changing hay, and shoveling sh—manure. It wasn't much of a job, but I was a hard worker and by the end of my first week I was cinching up saddles and hitchin' wagons for the boarders.

"That was where I met Meriwa. She was a young Tlingit girl, dark and slim, with eyes black as a moonless midnight. The first time I saw her was from my window one night after work. She liked to come to town and listen to the piano music that drifted from the saloon where I had rented a room for the time being. She was across the street, swaying in the shadows to that old out-of-tune piano. I cleaned myself up as best I could, washed some of the smell of the stable off me and changed my clothes, then went down to talk to her. Her English was fair, better than my Tlingit. I was instantly smitten. She seemed mysterious to me. Magical.

"After that first night I took every opportunity to be around Meriwa. She was friendly and seemed eager to talk about just about anything. She told me she was *Kaagwaantaan* clan, or Wolf clan as we'd call it. Also, that she was apprenticing as a medicine woman. I found her to be endlessly fascinating as well as beautiful and I realized I was swiftly falling in love. Unfortunately, Meriwa didn't feel the same way. I tried wooing her in every way I knew how—which wasn't much, honestly. But she had no interest in me romantically. However, she remained friendly, and I continued to spend time with her, although for me it was becoming bittersweet.

"One day she surprised me with a gift—this pipe. I never told your Pa who I got it from, just that I got it from some Tlingit Indians, but it was from Meriwa. She had hand-carved it from whale bone. I asked her what was the occasion for such a gift and she told me we were *ax̱ x̱oonx'i yán*—friends. That's all. Well, I was taken aback. Such a beautiful gift, made by her own hands, just for me."

Outside, the wailing sound was growing louder. It raised goosebumps on my skin to hear it, but Grandpa Jake didn't seem to take any notice of it at all. He kept his eyes lowered and carried on with his story.

"I was overcome with emotion for her. I looked at her sittin' there, those dark, almond-shaped eyes all lit up, her sweet, sensuous mouth smilin' at me. Without thinking, I leaned over and tried to kiss her. She was surprised and pushed me away. Somethin' inside me started to bubble up and I tried to grab her, to wrap my arms around her, but she slapped my face and ran away. But before she ran, I saw the hurt in her eyes—the betrayal. I felt a wash of emotions, not all of 'em in sympathy with each other. Shame 'n frustration, anger 'n guilt, sadness 'n…well, somethin' more.

"Next thing I knew, I found myself in the saloon. I wasn't never really a drinkin' man, even in my youth, but that day and on into the evening I spent my week's pay on whiskey, tryin' to kill all those emotions. At some point, I was joined by a woman I'd seen in the saloon before as I passed through on the way to my room or to work and I bought her drinks as well. Before long, she had me up in her room. I was too naive back then to know what this woman's line of work was, but I found out that evening as we fell drunkenly onto her bed, and she started to get me out of my clothes. When she was naked, too, she climbed on top of me, and I was so drunk I couldn't think straight, and I gasped out Meriwa's name. The woman looked at me, surprised, and then burst into laughter. I was instantly mad and demanded to know what was so funny. She began mocking me for 'fantasizin' about that filthy Indian witch'. I asked her what she meant by that, and she said that Meriwa was known in these parts as a heathen enchantress and no God-fearing white man in his right mind would have anything to do with her. I told her she was crazy, but she just kept laughin' and callin' Meriwa all kinds of vile names, accusin' her of witchcraft. I tried to get her to stop and get back to what we'd been intending, but I wasn't in any kind of mood for it anymore and that was readily apparent, which just made her laugh harder and start mockin' my wilted manhood. I was boilin' by this time and threw her off the bed so hard she cracked her head against the wall, which finally shut her up. I jumped up and got dressed quickly and fled the room.

"I was so drunk...wasn't thinkin' clearly at all. My mind was just a haze of anger and humiliation. That don't justify what happened next, mind you. I ain't makin' excuses. But damn it, boy, I've been livin' with this for a goddamn long time, and I've got to get it out. I stumbled out of the saloon feeling a mix of rage and something else which I didn't understand just then, but it was the *almost*, if you know what I mean. See, I had never been with a woman before and here I had just a few minutes ago had a naked, willing woman astride me, but it hadn't happened...just *almost*. My thoughts were all mixed-up and I was full of feelings I had never experienced before. Anger, lust, rejection, love...or what I thought was love...clouded my mind and it...it made me crazy, boy. Crazy! Don't you see?"

Grandpa Jake actually gave a little laugh, like he couldn't hear at all the eerie sounds surrounding our cabin that had now been joined by an ominous scraping across the wooden deck of our back porch, like something sharp being dragged across the boards. I cast a glance over my shoulder at the dark hallway, wondering if this infernal noise would soon bring Mama and the girls.

A terrible caterwauling erupted out on the back porch that set Charlie to his feet from where he'd been nervously drowsing by the fire and got him growling his warning growl deep in his throat. I reached over and crooked my arm around his neck and could feel his muscles straining as he leaned toward the door. I glanced at Grandpa Jake, but he once again seemed lost in another world, another time, not taking notice of me or Charlie or the ruckus on the back porch or the rising moans and wails that were swirling around on the wind. And much louder than Charlie's growls, I could hear the most awful snorting, slobbering sounds right outside our door, while the boards of the porch creaked and groaned alarmingly.

Grandpa Jake held up the bone pipe and I noticed a tremor in his hands. Now there was such a pandemonium outside that I knew Mama and the girls would be out here in a moment to see what was going on. But I had to know how this story ended and I silently willed Grandpa Jake to continue.

"I went lookin' for Meriwa. In my muddled mind I intended to profess my love to her one last time. Somehow, I knew, just *knew*, that this time she'd finally see that we were meant for each other. That thought got fixed in my head to the point that I didn't see there was any other way for things to play out. Well, I found her strolling along the seashore under the moonlight, in the woods just down from her clan's village. She heard me crashing through the brush and looked up. Her eyes were wide with surprise and a smile started to spread across her face, but it stopped as I got closer and the surprise in her eyes turned to fear. I say that now, looking back, but at the time I was out of my head. My mouth opened and words started pouring out—I don't know what they were or if I was makin' any sense. She started to back away from me and I reached out quick and grabbed her. Suddenly, all those earlier ideas I had were gone. All that remained inside me was rage and lust. Next thing I knew I had pulled Meriwa to the ground an' held her there. I remember feeling my hardness against her bare thigh and fumbling with the buttons on my trousers while crushing her to the ground with my whole weight. She struggled at first and without thinkin' my fist lashed out and struck her and then I felt her body go limp as I forced myself inside her. I looked at her face and she was starin' straight at me, her dark eyes filled with hate. I couldn't take it and looked away, but I didn't stop what I was doin' until I was spent. It didn't take long. A few awkward thrusts and I felt myself release inside her.

"Shame instantly flooded over me. I jumped up and ran, holdin' up my trousers, crashing through the brush and runnin' into trees, I was so drunk, and my eyes were so blurred with tears. I didn't stop til I got back to town, and when I did, I seen there was a ruckus at the saloon. That bar-wench had gone and riled up the patrons and I realized they was lookin' for me. So, I crept around the edge of town to the livery and then hid myself up in the hay loft. I must've passed out up there, for when I poked my head up out of the hay, I saw it was about sunrise. I climbed down out of the loft and took a peek outside. The town was quiet, and the saloon was dark. I was able to slip up to my room unnoticed. My head felt like it was full of rocks and my body ached almost as bad. I sat on the edge of my bed and contemplated my situation. It would have been a blessed mercy if I had had no memory of my actions that night, but they were there and they wouldn't stop tormentin' me. It was a pain deep in my soul, and way worse than any hangover, which I'd find out in the following years as I tried to drink away my misery. I knew my time in Chilkoot was done. I was about to pack up and leave town when I saw the bone pipe Meriwa had carved for me sittin' on the little table next to my bed. I picked it up and the tears come to my eyes, and I knew I just couldn't up an' leave without tryin' to talk to Meriwa. To find out if she was alright. To ask her forgiveness. So, I snuck back out of the saloon and headed back to the scene of my misdeed. I'm not sure why I didn't go straight to her village or look for her somewheres else. It just seemed like I had to go back to that spot. Of course, she wasn't there. But what was there was a big granite rock, and on that rock scrawled in blood—*her* blood, I was sure—was a phrase that's been burned into my brain all these years: *chush yáa akg̱wasnéi*. I didn't know what it meant then, but I learned it soon enough: *she will get even with him*.

"I turned around and left right then and there. I no longer wanted to see Meriwa, I just wanted to disappear. But I could never forget what I'd done, no matter how much whiskey I poured down my throat.

"It was almost immediately that the dreams started to come. Every night I saw Meriwa's face looming out of the darkness, her black eyes reflecting the dancing flames that surrounded her. She chanted words I didn't understand, but like that bloody phrase on the rock they burned into my brain and gave me the terrors. And behind her I could see somethin'; a huge, bestial shape, pacing like it was the livin' embodiment of a barely contained hatred. Every night the dreams came and every morning I woke up tremblin', covered in sweat.

"After weeks of this, I couldn't stand it no more. It was on Vancouver Island that I went to a local shaman to ask for help. He was the one told me that I was being cursed by a *naak'w s'aati.* And finally, I knew that everything that woman in Chilkoot had accused Meriwa of was true. She *was* a witch. And according to this shaman she was plenty powerful to be able to cast herself into my dreams like that, and her bein' so young, that power was just goin' to grow and grow."

It was getting darker outside, and I had to glance at the clock over the stove to remind myself that it was still morning. I was thinkin' about Mama and Sallie and little Baby Lynn in the back room—why hadn't Mama come out yet to check on that noise?—when a terrible knocking began on the door; a steady *thump*, *thump*, *thump* that made the hair on my arms stand up. Grandpa Jake wasn't looking so day-dreamy anymore, but kind of pale and trembly. He was lightly tapping that pipe against the table again. I reached over and put my hand over his and he looked up and met my eyes.

"Guess I better finish this story," he said.

III. REVENGE OF THE WITCH

Before he could get out another word a round of bone-chilling howls erupted from outside and I heard Sallie scream and Baby Lynn begin to cry. I jumped up and ran into the back room. What I saw chilled my heart. Mama lay on the floor, unmoving, her wide-open eyes glassed over like that stuffed wildcat Billy Ray's pa has mounted over their fireplace. I knelt down and felt her face; it was cold. I rested my head against her breast and heard her heart beating, though. Sallie was cradling Baby Lynn who was still crying.

"What happened?" I said.

"She—she just fell over," Sallie said, lower lip trembling. "Is she—?"

"She's alive," I said, "But—"

I didn't finish the sentence because I saw something out of the corner of my eye. I turned my head to the window and saw a face, blurred by the frost, looking in at us. Just for a second, then it was gone. But it had been there long enough for me to see the long, black hair—tangled and wild—and the black, almond-shaped eyes.

Just then another round of savage pounding sent me running back to the kitchen. Grandpa Jake was standing with his Remington aimed toward the door and Charlie beside him, trembling and growling. The door was positively bulging inward as something crashed against it with tremendous force.

"Grandpa Jake, what's happening?" I screamed.

"She's found me, boy. I'm sorry. I'm so sorry I brought this on y'all." He took his eyes off the door long enough to shoot me a glance and I saw true pain staring through. I was about to reply but then the door burst open, and my voice dried up. I felt a stream of piss run down my leg and I 'bout to threw up my meager breakfast.

What stood in the doorway was a nightmare, no doubt about that. It was huge, standing almost to the top of the door, even on all fours. It was like a wolf, but its long, grizzled fur was pure white, and it had eyes that burned yellow. Its jagged teeth were bared, saliva dripping from its drawn-back black lips, and its breath shot out of its flaring nostrils. The white fur of its muzzle was flecked with red. It took me a second to realize that the red was blood—fresh blood—and then the monster moved, and I saw the body that lay beneath it, mangled and torn. I tried to scream but nothing came out. Charlie, God bless 'em, tried to lunge forward, but I fell on him and stopped him before he could get hisself kilt.

"Get outta here!" Grandpa Jake shouted. He lifted the rifle and I saw his finger tighten on the trigger, but then she stepped in front of the giant wolf-thing. I saw immediately that hers was the face I'd just seen at the window, and I knew somehow that she was the one caused Mama to fall asleep like that. At least, I hoped she was just asleep.

"You've no business here," Grandpa Jake said. "I've repented of my sin a thousand times over. Let me be."

The woman—Meriwa, for I knew now for a certainty that that's who she was—said nothing, just stared with black hatred at Granda Jake. But then she turned those dark eyes on me. Without turning away, she gestured to the giant beast, and it lowered its muzzle to the body beneath it. Those dagger-teeth sank into the flesh and lifted the body so that I saw my Pa's poor bloody face as his head lolled around like Sallie's rag doll.

Then Meriwa spoke and her voice was like if a snake could speak. Though she was still staring at me she was talking to Grandpa Jake. "A trade, Jake McCollough. Pay your price or they all will suffer for your sin."

Grandpa Jake was trembling, and his aim was poor when he finally pulled the trigger. His shot went wild, and the witch laughed when the glass of the window next to the door burst out. I couldn't tell much difference between her laugh and the shattering glass.

"Bitch!" Grandpa Jake screamed. "Leave me be! I came back, didn't I? Back to tell you how goddamn sorry I was!"

Meriwa laughed that broken-glass laugh again. "And then you ran, Jake McCollough. You ran like a coward. Now I offer you redemption." Again, she gestured to the beast, which shook its head making my Pa's body flop around like a puppet. "Pay your price or your sin will end them all."

Those black eyes were still locked on me and suddenly I realized what the witch was offering; either Grandpa Jake went with her willingly or she'd kill us all. I didn't know if my pa was already dead, but I knew Sallie and Baby Lynn were alive and Mama, although I didn't know what kind of spell she was under, was still breathing, too. I looked at Grandpa Jake, but he just stood there, rooted to the floor.

“Grandpa Jake,” I started. But I didn’t know what else to say. Beneath me, I felt Charlie’s muscles still tensed to spring.

He looked at me, his eyes wide with fright, lower lip trembling. “I can’t, boy,” he whispered. “I—I love you, but I can’t…”

Meriwa finally took her eyes off me and turned to Grandpa Jake. “Still a coward, Jake McCollough. And for that, you’ll be the last to die.”

I saw her hand about to lift toward the beast again and the words of my pa flashed through my mind, *You’re the man of the house now, Joseph. I want you to take care of your ma and sisters. Protect them. At any cost.*

That scream finally found its way out of my throat as I jumped up from Charlie and ran up behind Grandpa Jake and shoved him hard toward the door. He dropped his rifle as he stumbled forward, arms flailing. Meriwa smiled as the creature dropped my pa’s limp body and opened its jaws wide just in time for Grandpa Jake to fall right into ‘em.

I turned away, but not quick enough to miss those jaws crunch through my grandfather’s chest and a fresh spray of blood cover the beast’s muzzle. Grandpa Jake moaned and Meriwa laughed, and I sank to my knees, covering my ears so as not to hear any of it. I felt Charlie come up beside me and felt his breath on my face. I wrapped my arms around him and sobbed. "Damn you," I cried, "damn you." I didn't know if I sayin' it to Meriwa or to my grandfather.

The wolf-thing took my grandfather off toward the woods, leaving a sickening trail of blood and clumps of things I didn't want to think about. Hot tears spilled down my cheeks as I tried to wake myself up from this terrible nightmare.

Then I felt her standing over me. I looked up, ready for that creature to bite off my head, but it was gone. The witch pointed to my pa's body. I shook my head, but she scowled and pointed again. I got up slowly, leaving Charlie whimpering on the floor, and went to the doorway. I knelt down and touched Pa's face. It was cold. So cold. And scratched and bloody. But I felt breath coming from his nostrils. I started crying again, as I struggled to drag his body across the floor to the fireplace.

Meriwa stood in the doorway as if waiting for something. I couldn't figure at first what she wanted; she'd got my grandpa, got her revenge for what he did to her. I had a flash of panic at the thought that she'd been lying, that we were all gonna die, anyway, but then I remembered something. I got up and went to the table, picked up Grandpa Jake's bone pipe and took it to Meriwa. I held it out to her, and she took it and put it inside her shirt. Then she turned and, on bare feet, followed the red trail into the woods.

Sallie ran into the room with Baby Lynn, saw Pa and burst into tears.

"Pa! What happened Joe? What happened?"

I knew what had happened, of course, but how could I even begin to explain it to her. A moment later, those dang tears started flowing again when I saw Mama walk unsteadily into the room like she'd just woke up, which I guess she had.

Well, not much left to tell, I guess. We got Pa up and cleaned off and warm and he appeared to be mostly okay. He bore some ragged scars for the rest of his days but blessedly he had no memory of what had happened.

As for Grandpa Jake...well, as I was the only one who really knew the truth, I told everyone that our home had been attacked by a pack of starving wolves and that Grandpa Jake had tried to fight 'em off but they was just too many and too savage for him. Said I stayed to guard Mama and Sallie and Baby Lynn. It wasn't much of a story, but it was the best I could do. When Pa was healed and getting his strength back, me 'n' him went out into the woods to see if we could find any trace of Grandpa Jake. I knew we wouldn't, but I did it for Pa.

I don't know if Grandpa Jake was a bad man, or a man that just did a bad thing and thought he could outlive it. But I think those deeds come back to haunt us if we don't put 'em right. And in the end, they destroy us.

Sepulcro de Demonios

El Lobo Gordo sped his Cadillac into the cemetery, slinging dust and gravel. The iron gates of the graveyard groaned at his passing. He brought the car to a grinding halt against his grandfather's tombstone, the bumper kissing the engraved letters of Grandfather's name. El Lobo Gordo adjusted his mask, wiped sweat from his thick neck and got out of the car. The Cadillac rose three inches as El Lobo Gordo's bulk was removed. The masked man stood in the swirling dust of his own tempest and surveyed the cemetery. It was el Día de los Muertos and he had come to defend his grandsire against the hordes of hell.

The little goat looked up from cropping its patch of brown grass just as El Lobo Gordo's giant booted foot crunched a piece of granite mere inches from its nose. The shabby beast coughed a grunt of irritation. El Lobo Gordo ignored the creature and sat down on a tombstone to light a cigarette. He pulled his mask over his large, slick lips. They clamped the cigarette the way El Lobo Gordo's mighty thighs had squeezed El Toro Hermoso into submission, cracking six ribs in the process. El Lobo Gordo smiled at the memory. He struck a match on the tombstone and lit the cigarette, inhaling deeply.

Grandfather Luchador had not yet been in his grave on the last Day of the Dead, only lying in terrible fever-ridden sickness. For sixty-seven years, he had practiced the black arts—like his ancestors before him—conjuring and controlling demons, holding them captive by blood and smoke and sacred incantations, making them do his bidding. The enslaved demons, so near to release, were lurking near his deathbed with a hideous soul-hunger. Only Grandmother La Rosa Mágica, with her own witchery, was able to hold off the demons and keep them from devouring her beloved husband's spirit. But now Grandfather Luchador was susceptible to demonic attack, as his soul once again visited this plane, as did all the souls on this, the day of their honor.

The sun was setting; shadows of crosses and angels' wings stretching toward El Lobo Gordo like dark, deformed fingers. The goat came close and lay down next to El Lobo Gordo's great, booted foot, tucking its stubby-horned head under a cloven hoof. El Lobo Gordo could feel the little creature trembling. He reached down and stroked it absently as his eyes scanned the darkening cemetery. His lips puffed on the cigarette and smoke curled around his head like a polluted halo. A breeze slithered through the tombstones sending a ripple of gooseflesh across El Lobo Gordo's brawny shoulders. Clad only in his tights, the creeping cold of evening was all too apparent to the huge wrestler. His cape was still in the Cadillac, but El Lobo Gordo was hesitant to fetch it – it hindered one's movement in a fight.

"Baaaahhhhhh!"

The little goat suddenly shot up from its resting place next to El Lobo Gordo's boot and stood quaking with fear. El Lobo Gordo tore the cigarette from his lips and threw it into a waiting grave nearby. He pulled his mask down over his mouth, hiding the fierce grin that crept across his face. It would come early then. Fine, thought El Lobo Gordo, I hate waiting around.

The last of the daylight was fading. Against the silhouette of a terrifying, skeletal Christ, an obscene yellow moon rose like the eye of some great, lethargic beast. The shadows pulled and stretched and pointed in impossible directions. El Lobo Gordo's head spun with disorienting perspective. Tombs were erupting. The whole graveyard was in a state of upheaval. El Lobo Gordo bit down hard on the inside of his cheek, tasting blood and causing his vision to blur with tears. But the pain cleared his head. The ground was stable again and the shadows straightened. But now El Lobo Gordo's hearing was assaulted with piercing shrieks. His powerful hands clamped against his ears, but they could not keep out the hideous wailing. Suddenly demons were upon him. El Lobo Gordo felt their claws scraping across his flesh, freezing the blood in his veins. The demon's breath stank and burned his nostrils. He let out a barbaric yell and flung his mighty arms out with all his force, scattering the clinging phantoms. They dissipated upon the wind like dark smoke from a chimney then reassembled themselves into their horrid forms and attacked again. The demons were relentless and the strength of El Lobo Gordo, although legendary, was not infinite. The great wrestler began to tire as the screeching demons wore him down. All around him, the graveyard was exploding with the dead. Corpses clutched at their heads, many bony fingers searching for ears that no longer existed, to stop the noise of the hellish invaders as it echoed inside their skulls.

"Desecrators!" shouted El Lobo Gordo. His tights were bloody rags; his mask clung to his head in tatters. Around El Lobo Gordo, the shadow-demons gathered in a menacing circle. The cemetery was eerily silent now; the wind had died, and the land lay still. The eyes of the demons glared with red hatred, lit inside by the very fires of Hell. El Lobo Gordo's shoulders sagged with weariness and sweat dripped from every pore of his gigantic body. His eyes scanned the ranks of demons as they stretched out their black, skeletal arms and claw met claw with a rasp like the last breath of a dying wretch. The circle of demons grew tighter…closer…

Suddenly, El Lobo Gordo's huge chest heaved with exertion. His fists, now useless against the hellish host, clenched tightly at his sides. The wrestler's great lungs inhaled deeply, powerfully. The eyes of the demons grew wide with confusion and curiosity. Then, when the realization dawned on them, it was too late…

El Lobo Gordo drew the very air around him into his mighty lungs and the phantoms that surrounded him were caught like a sinking ship in a whirlpool. They had advanced too closely to El Lobo Gordo and were now prisoners of the unrelenting vacuum that he had become. His face turned red under his mask with the effort of keeping up the continuous inhalation; his lungs burned, and his veins stood out from his trembling arms like writhing snakes. But El Lobo Gordo did not give in.

He felt the first phantasm slide past his lips and into his body, felt its shriek as it struggled not to be absorbed. But it was no use. El Lobo Gordo inhaled the smoky creature and felt it subside as it entered his body. The other demons were consumed in turn, with considerable screaming and howling. But the great wrestler was undaunted. Indeed, a savage strength seemed to have been imbued in him; a strength that grew with each consumed demon. When the entire host was gone from the graveyard and everything was peaceful once more, then did El Lobo Gordo allow himself to collapse upon the ground in fatigue.

Around him, the newly risen dead crawled toward him. The remains of El Lobo Gordo's ancestors comforted the man as best they could; keeping him company while the bloated, yellow moon crept across the sky over the graveyard. In the night, El Lobo Gordo woke and stared up at the moon. Far off in the distance he heard the yipping of a lonesome coyote. He sat up and looked around. He was alone. The graveyard was awash in moonlight and the sepulchers shone brightly white underneath the lunar light. The graves did not appear to have been disturbed. El Lobo Gordo could not say the same for himself, however. He ponderously got to his feet and shuffled through the dust to his Cadillac. He reached inside, opened the glove compartment, and removed a cigarette, which he stuck between his lips. He struck a match and stood in the orange glare for a second, thinking. And the doctors tell me I should quit smoking. He smiled and lit the cigarette, savoring the acrid smoke as it filled his lungs.

As he climbed behind the wheel of the Cadillac, El Lobo Gordo thought he heard the sound of coughing and retching, but from far off, as if carried on the wind. Then the sound was lost in the revving of the Cadillac's engine and the roar of gravel underneath its tires as the wrestler sped away into the night, his once-yearly familial obligation finished.

* * *

In the desert wind hear the victory cry of El Lobo Gordo, Mexico's greatest wrestler.

"Ay-ay-ay!!! I have won over my enemy!"

Ashes to Ashes

Sleep was a distant memory and daylight a half-remembered dream.

Ben lay tangled in grimy sheets on the bed that he had come to loathe during these past sweltering, restless nights and watched a fly crawl across the ceiling with excruciating slowness. With an effort, he hunched up on one elbow to check the time. 6:15 a.m. If he were sleeping, he could doze for another half-hour or so before getting up and getting ready for work. But there was no sleep and there was no work.

He rose from the rumpled bed. Stumbling to the window, he leaned on the sill with his forehead pressed up against the glass and looked out upon the town below him. It lay silent and deserted underneath a smudged charcoal drawing of a sky. The streets and housetops were covered with what looked like filthy grey snow and more was falling from the sky. Ben wrenched open the window, stuck his arm out and let the flakes fall on his skin. They were hot to the touch, but the sensation roused him, made him more alert. He made a fist, tightened the muscles in his forearm until his veins stood out angrily and surrendered his flesh to the burning snow.

Twilight at dawn. Even if he hadn't been semi-delirious from the heat and lack of sleep it would still have been disorienting. The sun was a raw, red bullet wound on the horizon and what light it gave was feeble and disquieting.

Ben pulled his arm back in and shut the window. He wandered into the bathroom and ran cold water into the sink. While the basin filled, he went to the shower and touched the clothes she had left hanging on the shower rod to dry. Two pairs of jeans, a dress, a pair of leggings and her Wonder Woman panties. As much as he would have loved—and needed—a shower, he was not able to bring himself to remove her things. Instead, he went back to the sink, dipped his hands into the water and splashed it on his face and bare chest. The water dripped down his body and pooled on the floor. Shutting off the faucet, he stood in the already tepid water while he studied his face in the mirror. His skin was sallow and sagging, as if he'd borrowed a face from someone else. Black half-moons hung beneath his bloodshot eyes. Grey stubble sprouted from his jaw like mold. He reached over for a washcloth, dipped it in the sink and wiped the sweat off the rest of his body.

He went back into the other room, still wet and naked, and checked the clock. 6:30. He looked out the window again. If anything, it seemed a little bit darker. He wandered back to his bed and collapsed onto it, deeply exhausted. On the little bedside table, next to the alarm clock, was a framed picture of her, taken by himself on the last date they had together. His fingers reached out and touched the picture, then slid slowly down, leaving a streak on the glass.

Christ, he was already sweating again.

Scrounging around the studio apartment, Ben eventually located a pair of semi-clean pants, an acceptable shirt and two clean socks. The socks didn't match, but no matter. He put on the clothes and then got his boots from the closet.

Outside, the air burned his lungs. He tied a bandana around his mouth and nose and breathed as infrequently as possible, taking tiny sips of air. The fires had been raging for weeks and were now just a few miles away. Ben could see the orange glow licking the sky in the distance. The foothills of the Cascade Mountain range glowed as if infested with a thousand fecund fireflies. It was eerily silent and still. A sepia haze hung over everything. No wind, no bird calls. All the animals had mostly likely fled the area already, along with the rest of the townsfolk.

The ash falling from the leaden sky steadily increased. It gathered on his shoulders and in his hair. He left footprints behind him as he made his way down the block. When he caught glimpses of himself in windows as he passed, he was startled to see a ragged scarecrow.

When Ben reached the hardware store, he paused a moment before unlocking the door, looking back toward the glowing mountains, squinting his eyes against the gloom. Something was moving in all that smoke up in the hills. Something dark and amorphous. Something Ben had been keeping an eye on for days.

He watched it now, as the shadow rose above the smoke and cast about as if trying to catch his scent.

It was coming for him.

Ben went inside the store, removed the bandanna and flicked on the lights, turning on the neon "We're Open" sign. It was fortunate that the electricity was still working, but he didn't expect it to last much longer.

The hardware store wasn't his. He had never actually set foot in it before the fires and the town's evacuation. The day after everyone left, he had been wandering around aimlessly and happened to see that there was a set of keys jutting from the lock on the door. He tried the keys, the door opened, and he went inside. This was also fortunate—there were things in here he could use, things he needed. And it beat laying around in the relentless heat of his studio apartment. The store had air conditioning at least. For now.

He sat on a stool behind the cash register, reading the last printed issue of the town newspaper. The editor of the paper was gone, now, along with the rest of the staff. Also, the barber, the folks who worked at the Safeway, the gas station attendants, the dentist, the doctor, his drug dealer, and every other citizen of the town.

Everyone except Ben.

The headline of the newspaper he was reading to tatters was, of course, about the fires—three separate conflagrations that were spreading, getting closer to each other and threatening to become one enormous inferno, hungrily devouring as much land as possible. Three towns had already been consumed and Ben's was next in its path if it remained unchecked. There were several companies of beleaguered and exhausted firefighters battling the blaze, but he was not optimistic as to their chances.

Ben opened the paper and spread it across the counter. He glanced at a shorter story on page three. The scanty details were by now burned into his brain. His mind involuntarily filled in the gaps of the story where police had only been speculating. The article was accompanied by a grainy, black and white picture of a young woman; the same picture that was back in his apartment, but with all the color leached out. She was smiling, a few strands of her shoulder-length blonde hair caught in time as a breeze blew them across her face. Her eyes were so bright, so *alive*. Ben traced his finger along her jawline where the paper was worn smooth from previous delineations.

After a while, he stood up and stretched. He folded the newspaper and placed it beneath the counter. The store had provided the tools he needed, but he hadn't realized how long it would take to finish his task and time was running short. He grabbed a few back up items—extra gloves, more rope—and tossed them into the wheelbarrow, which he had also liberated from the store. Ben tied the bandana around his nose and mouth and then wheeled his way out into the street and down another few blocks. The sky had barely lightened since he'd been inside, and even more ash was falling. He glanced toward the hills and saw the shadow moving through the smoke and blackened pines. He quickly looked away.

Ben parked the wheelbarrow at the automatic doors of the supermarket, which were stuck partially open. The wheelbarrow itself wouldn't fit through the doors, but there was enough room for Ben to slip inside. He picked up a hand basket and walked down the aisles, not thinking, just blinking against the glare of the fluorescent lights. On aisle seven he picked a package of chocolate chip cookies off the shelf, ripped open the bag and numbly munched on one beneath the bandana. His footsteps rang hollowly on the tile, echoing through the empty store, accentuating his solitude. In the artificial light, his eyes were playing tricks on him. Shapes wavered dimly at the ends of aisles; shadows leaned toward him where no objects stood. He rubbed at his eyes, ate another cookie, and continued gathering items. The basket filled up with bags of potato chips, a loaf of bread, a jar of peanut butter, a six-pack of Coke and several bottles of water. When he couldn't fit any more into the basket, Ben headed back to the wheelbarrow.

As he stepped through the broken doors the air struck him with a thick, dirty heat. Even through the bandana he could smell the smoke; the charred remains of the life the fire was consuming. His eyes were dry and irritated, almost as red as the bloody sun floating through the grimy haze above. The air was oppressive and stifling. The smoke wound around buildings, streetlamps, trees, and billboards like filthy translucent tentacles. More shapes and shadows leered out of the smog; dark alien visages, malevolent features hungrily following him—the last living being—with malicious intent.

There were lights and noises in the sky. A dark shape slashed its way through the smoke and debris overhead. Ben felt a pounding, painful pressure on his eardrums. He dropped to his knees and wrapped his arms around his head until it passed.

When it was quiet again, he tentatively sat up and tried to orient himself. He shook his head vigorously until his vision seemed a little clearer. A helicopter. It had only been one of the helicopters that periodically flew over town. They sent them out from McChord Air Force Base near Tacoma, taking either gallons of water or more firefighters out into the conflagration.

He got up, steadied himself, and grabbed a can of Coke. He popped it open and chugged half its contents. The caffeine and sugar would give him a boost of artificial energy until he finished the job.

Ben set the basket of goods next to the other items and then walked over to the freezer outside the store where they kept bags of ice. He stood in front of the freezer looking at the cartoon penguin sledding between giant snowflakes and the word ICE with icicles dripping off the letters in case you didn't already get the point. There had been a padlock on the doors when Ben first got the idea to use the freezer. That had been the first time the hardware store had proven useful. A pair of bolt-cutters made quick work of the lock. It still lay on the ground, useless, where Ben had left it. Now he unconsciously kicked it aside as he grasped the handles of the freezer doors. He was about to pull them open when he remembered the wheelbarrow was still over by the main doors. Sighing deeply, he walked back to the items he had laid aside, swallowed down the rest of the can of Coke and then pushed the wheelbarrow back over to the freezer. He maneuvered it under the doors, grasped the handles once again and pulled.

Her body lay nestled among the bags of the ice, her exposed skin a limpid blue with a delicate spider-web tracing of veins beneath. Here and there angry purple bruises disturbed the icy serenity of her otherwise pallid flesh, the most vivid circling her throat. Her blonde hair glittered with frost and her still open eyes were rimed with white crystals. When Ben lifted her into the wheelbarrow, he winced at the ripping sound as the plastic bags of ice tore away from her body. He piled the other items around her as respectfully as he could and then turned the wheelbarrow away from the store and, putting his full weight behind it, began pushing.

As he trundled the wheelbarrow down the street, Ben felt the baleful presence of the shadow drawing nearer. He was almost at a run, sweat pouring into his already stinging eyes, blurring his vision even further. Soon he left the stores and houses of the town behind him. In their place, dark pines reached up into the thickening smoke. Some of the trees grew in shallow earth and, in the gloom, their exposed roots looked like knotted piles of snakes. Ben concentrated on the road before him, but he saw shapes moving peripherally in the smoke, between the pines. Each breath was now agony. He sobbed in relief when he finally reached his destination.

Ben pushed the wheelbarrow through the cemetery gates and fell to his knees. He stayed that way, head bowed to the earth, for a few minutes, struggling to breathe in the increasing heat and smoke. Finally, he heaved himself up and grabbed another Coke. He swigged from the can as he opened one of the bags of chips and then made himself a rudimentary sandwich. When he had eaten and finished the cola, Ben reached back into the wheelbarrow and as gently as he could pulled the items away from her body. Next to the wheelbarrow was the casket he had taken from the town's funeral home. He had loaded it into his truck and driven it out here, but on the way back to his apartment the truck had run out of gas and Ben just left it in the street. That's when he thought of the wheelbarrow. The physical exertion would be a kind of penance before the ending came.

Ben put on his gloves, surveyed the grave he had been digging for the past couple of days—ever since the last of the townsfolk had cleared out and he had been able to come out of hiding. He grabbed the pickaxe, lowered himself into the grave and laid into the earth with grim determination. When he had churned up enough dirt he switched to the shovel and tossed the soil aside. He alternated like this for a while. By late afternoon, Ben was shirtless, sweating, fatigued, and filthy. He only allowed himself to rest long enough to drink more Coke and fortify himself with sandwiches before starting back to work. When the hole was deep enough, Ben rigged up the rope and bucket to haul the dirt out, using a tombstone as a makeshift lever. This made excavation easier but slowed him down even more. Exhaustion was setting in, but he tapped a deep reserve of strength, and after another hour or so the grave was finally finished. He hoisted himself out with the rope and then collapsed, his muscles in knots and dark spots dancing before his eyes.

The sky above him was dark and undulated in loathsome billows. Embers mixed with the falling ash. Ben pushed himself up on his elbows and saw the fire fully. The hills were engulfed with flame, and it was spreading with ferocious speed.

Forcing himself up, Ben went back to the wheelbarrow and roughly dragged her body into the coffin. His mind screamed against the lack of respect accorded the body, but his stamina was waning, and he still had to get the casket into the grave. Before he shut the lid, Ben's finger traced the curve of the girl's jaw line. His eyes briefly flickered to the bruises around her throat and then quickly looked away. He bent over her and kissed the blue lips.

"I am truly sorry." He wasn't sure if he said the words out loud and wasn't sure if it mattered.

Using the rope-and-tombstone pulley system he had devised for the bucket; Ben used his last remaining strength to maneuver the box into the ground and then shoveled the dirt back over the coffin until the hole was filled. Stripping off his gloves, he fell on top of the grave and lost consciousness.

* * *

Ben opened his eyes and saw Hell descending.

Beyond the stone walls of the cemetery, fire raged uncontrollably. He held his arm up over his face against the heat and the glare and squinted into the flames, looking for the shadow that had been relentlessly stalking him. He stood up, slowly, every muscle in his body screaming in agony. Staggering toward the gates, Ben tried to remember the events that had led to this. All that came were shattered fragments, bits of half-remembered emotions: confusion, disbelief, rage, remorse, sorrow, guilt. But none of them would fit together. One memory would begin to connect to another, but then it would slide away, like a fish that almost went for the bait but sensed the hook and turned at the last moment, fading into the murky depths of his mind.

At the gates, Ben stopped and leaned against the black iron bars. He watched, fascinated, as across the road the needles on the pine trees began to smolder and smoke and then burst into flame. He pushed off from the gates, staggered into the middle of the road and stood with arms outstretched, facing the coming conflagration.

“Here I am,” he whispered through cracked lips. He wanted to cry, but his eyes were boiled dry by the heat.

The flames consumed the pines and then began to lick at the road. Ben saw the asphalt bubble and crack beneath his feet. Chunks of the road were now burning. The ash and embers fell around him like red rain, and he turned his face up to the stinging debris, relishing the pain. The fire was spreading rapidly toward him. Within the churning smoke a gargantuan shadow strode purposefully forward.

Ben’s blackening skin split from ear to ear as he smiled in anticipation of his retribution.

Monster in the Meadow

We raced through the meadow, upsetting the butterflies and sending dandelion seeds floating in the air all around us like tiny parachutes. Booney had them plastered around his big, slobbery mouth and on his tongue, which was always hanging out. Harvey and I couldn't seem to stop laughing. It was a carefree Saturday — a hot spring morning with the temperature already past the seventy-degree mark. We were anticipating the coming break from school. We were twelve.

At the bottom of the hill, Harvey lost his footing and tumbled through the grass, still laughing. I could have avoided him easily but instead, I crashed into him and did a flip through the air, landing on my back and knocking the wind out of me. When I got it back, I was still laughing, too. Booney came up short and sat in the grass, whacking the tall blades with his tail, looking at us like he did when he didn't really understand what was going on but wanted to join in anyway.

Harvey sat up and gave one last snorting laugh, then looked around like maybe he didn't know where he was. I think he was dizzy from the tumble. After a minute, he lowered himself back down into the grass with his arms beneath his head and his ankles crossed. I followed suit and we spent some time staring up into the blue-sky making pictures out of the wisps of clouds that periodically floated by. Booney threw himself down next to me and immediately fell asleep. I was just about drowsing off myself when we heard the cows over in the next pasture kicking up a ruckus.

"What the heck?" said Harvey, raising himself up a little on his elbows. We both looked out across the waves of brown grass and saw, on the other side of the rusty barbed-wire fence that ran the length of the pasture, a scrawny-looking coyote chasing the cows around and making a real clamor about it, too. The poor cows looked about scared to death—there isn't much that can rouse a cow when you think about it—and the coyote looked to be having the time of his life. Harvey said he didn't think that the coyote was going after food or anything, but just up to some fun. I agreed. We figured this fellow had gotten a little crazy from the unseasonable heat. While we were watching the coyote, Booney woke up from the noise and took off like a shot, thinking to get in on the excitement, I jumped up and ran after Booney, not wanting my dog to get in a tangle with a coyote, and Harvey leapt up and chased after me. Booney was barking for all he was worth, and Harvey and I were both yelling our heads off—those poor cows must've thought the world was coming to an end.

The coyote saw us coming and, true to form, slunk off quickly through the grass. We could see the wake he cut through the tall, brown stalks as he headed off toward the woods. Booney got tangled up in the herd of frightened cows and Harvey and I managed to collar him before he could go any further. We walked him back to the fence, me bent over funny from hanging on to Booney's collar and then plopped down on the ground to rest and sweat.

The fence sat on a low hill that looked out across Old Man Grover's pasture, which was kind of a shallow valley. A little ways off, about halfway to the woods, a good-sized pond offered the cows and birds and whatever else a nice waterin' hole. That's about all it was good for because it was always covered in a thin scum and had lily pads all over it, so it was no good for swimming. Besides, we had the river for that, and it was cleaner and colder.

This was the hottest spring we had ever had, and it had barely even begun. Already the farmers were talking drought when they came into town and hung around in Phil's barbershop, swapping stories and waiting to get their hair cut. Looking out over that valley we could see why they were talking that way. Already, that pond out there had gotten a little bit smaller. All my life, I'd only known that pond to get bigger and that was during the rainy season when it would spread out across half the pasture it seemed.

After the cows calmed down some, they started to head over to that pond to get a drink of water—that chase must've heated them up. But then the strangest thing happened. Those cows, the whole herd of them, stopped about twenty feet from the bank and lifted their noses in the air as if smelling something. Then they kind of shook their heads and turned around slowly the way cows do, and marched right back up the slight hill toward where we were sitting. It was then that Harvey noticed the things sticking up out of the water.

"Hey, Stan," he said, "Look at that." He pointed down at the pond and then I saw them, too. A row of what I thought at first must be fence posts, partially exposed due to the shrinking of the pond. They were brownish green, covered with slime and muck and moss. Most of them made a pretty neat row but a few leaned over to one side or the other. You couldn't see but the very tops of them though, and it was hard to judge how tall they were because nobody had ever actually been in the pond to find out how deep it was.

"What do you suppose those are?" I said, mostly speaking to myself.

"They look kinda like fence posts," said Harvey, echoing my thoughts.

"Yeah," I said, "never seen 'em before though. There's no fence runs that way across the field."

"Might'a been once, though. Who knows?"

We shrugged it off, as kids will do, and got up when we were rested enough and trekked back to town with Booney running along ahead of us. We met up with a bunch of the guys at the drugstore and got up a pretty fair game of baseball in the vacant lot on the edge of town that went on until dark. Even then we would've kept playing except Fuzzy Lester got hit on the head with a pop fly and started crying.

That night, I asked my dad about Old Man Grover's pasture and whether or not the pond had always been there or if there had been a fence running through there once. He told me that the pond had been there for as long as he remembered, which was quite a ways back. My dad had grown up in these parts before he went into the army and saw what lies beyond the county line. He came back to marry my mother though, and they settled here and then I came along. I guessed between the two of us we knew as much about the area as anyone, he said he didn't remember any fence running that way through the field, though, I forgot about the pond again and when it was time for bed I curled up under the covers with a flashlight and a copy of W*eird Tales* until I felt sleepy.

I woke up sweating and found I'd kicked my blankets off during the night. The sun was streaming in through the window and shadow leaves were dancing on my wall. I could tell it was going to be a wonderful day.

It was spring break, so school wasn't weighing on my mind the way it sometimes did. I was free to roam, and I planned on making the most of my vacation. I steam-shoveled breakfast, then hopped on my bike and pedaled over to Harvey's house with Booney running beside me all the way. But when I got there, Harvey's mom told me he'd been gone since about sunup and she wasn't sure where, but it must've been fishing because where else would someone go that early in the morning. I thanked her and got back on my bike trying to think where Harvey might be fishing. We had several spots that we called our "secret fishin' holes" although we never caught a darn thing in any of them and everybody else knew about them anyway. I decided to head out to the one down off the big rock, about a half-mile into the woods along the river.

The big rock was deserted so, one by one, I went to all our favorite spots. I was on my way out to the lake, passing Old Man Grover's pasture, when I just happened to look over and spotted Harvey sitting by himself on a fence post with his elbows on his knees and his head in his hands. I veered off the road and dropped my bike in the ditch, hopping off in one swift motion, and made my way through the long grass to where Harvey was sitting. Booney ran off after a pheasant that was flying low through the field.

"Where ya been?" I asked him, "You been sittin' here all morning?"

Harvey pointed down at the pond, never taking his eyes off it. “Look at that, will ya?"

I looked. The pond was definitely shrinking; you could see the muddy edges where the water used to reach. It was drying and cracking in the sun. I could smell something wafting up out of there but couldn't put any name to it. I thought about the cows the day before.

"You can see 'em a little better today," Harvey said. I could tell he was thinking about something; his forehead was all scrunched up into little lines.

“Those old fence posts?" I said. I had decided that that's what they were whether my dad remembered a fence there or not.

“I don't think those are fence posts, Stan," he said. "I think they're ... somethin' else.”

"What else could they be?" I asked.

Harvey lifted his head up and looked at me, “Let's go find out,” he said and jumped down off the post. He started off through the grass and what could I do but follow him?

The closer we got the stronger the smell came up at us. It wasn't exactly unpleasant, but it was strange and sort of familiar. I looked around for Booney but didn't see him anywhere so let him be for the time being. I caught up to Harvey and we walked down to the edge of the pond together. We stood on the bank and looked at the mud cracking in the sun. I lifted a foot and put a sneaker print in the mud then brought it out and wiped the bottom of my shoe on the grass. Flies were buzzing all around even though it was still early. I guessed it was because of the unseasonable heat.

"Look how they kinda raise up higher in the middle," Harvey said, illustrating with a gentle wave of his hand. "Then toward both ends, they get lower in the water until you can't see 'em anymore."

"There's probably a hill under the pond or somethin'," I said. For some reason, I felt a little scared. Not the kind of scared like when I thought Bill Whittaker was gonna beat the stuffing out of me at school that one time, but more like the kind of scared I got when I was reading *Weird Tales* or a Poe story, or watching a Karloff movie at the Bijou. A go*od* kind of scared.

"Nah," said Harvey, like he was a little disgusted with me, "I'm tellin' ya, Stan, those ain't fence posts."

Standing there that close to them, I had to agree that he was right. They were so covered with muck and green stuff and whatnot that it was hard to tell exactly what they were, but it was pretty obvious that they weren't wood, and they just weren't the right size to be any kind of fence post I'd ever seen. But what else could they be? Harvey acted like he knew but wasn't ready to give. I think he wanted me to figure it out and he was willing to wait until I did.

“Jeez!" I said. “If you're so smart, why don't *you* tell me what they are?”

Harvey looked around at me with a sly grin spreading over his freckled face. Let's come back tomorrow and see if the water's gone down a little more.

I could see I wasn't going to get anything else out of him and I was starting to become a little angry. I told myself that he didn't know what those things were any more than I did, but if he wanted to play like he did and come back tomorrow that was fine with me. In those days, we could make an adventure out of anything, and one thing was as good as another.

We walked back to the road, picked Booney up where I found him sleeping by my bike, and decided to go fishing after all. We walked over to Harvey's, me pushing my bike along out of consideration, and he got his pole and tackle box and his bike then we headed to my house, and I got my gear. We spent the rest of the day with our lines in the water, changing the worms every time they got too waterlogged to be any good. We talked about comics and movies and the H.G. Wells book I'd gotten at the library, and a little bit about Edna Parker who'd started getting breasts that year, but all along I knew we were both thinking about those strange things sticking up out of the water in Old Man Grover's Pond.

The fish must have seen us coming that day, they most always did it seemed, so eventually we packed it up and headed into town. We stopped at the drugstore and Harvey got a strawberry soda and I went for a root beer. They tasted real good on such a hot day. Then we pooled the rest of our money and bought a copy of a new comic book called *Weird Science.* It was probably the neatest comic either of us had ever read and it kept us entertained for most of the afternoon. We decided Harvey would take it home for the first week and then I could keep it the next since Harvey put in two cents more than I did.

Harvey had got me thinking about that pond and those strange things that were probably *not* fence posts. I racked my brain all night trying to come up with an explanation. We'd decided to keep an eye on that receding pond water though, then we'd see for sure.

Two or three days ran by, and the water got lower and lower all the time. We went out and checked the pond in the mornings and again in the evenings, just before we were expected back home for supper. We never went out at night though but stayed around town or at home. That's just the way it was we didn't generally go that far out at night because both of us had too many monster movies and horror stories cluttering up our heads to ever feel comfortable about it.

Anyway, every day that water line receded, and we could see a little more of whatever those things were, although it didn't help us much. There was so much muck and weeds dangling off them that we were starting to think that even if all the water was gone, we wouldn't be able to tell what they were. By the end of the week, Harvey was getting so impatient he suggested floating out there in a rowboat or something, pulling off some of those lily pads and moss streamers so we could just see everything and be done with it. But, for some reason, we were both a little scared to do that so we just kept coming out every morning and every evening and standing there on the muddy banks, all alone now because the cows had quit coming down the pasture that far, and talking quietly about what might be laying there under that pond.

On Saturday, Harvey had to go with his folks to visit his aunt in Portland and was gone all day. With my best friend out of town, my dad saw an opportunity to put me to work, so I spent all day cutting the grass and helping him paint the new shutters he'd put up for my mom. Harvey didn't get back till late, so we didn't get to check the pond at all that day.

Sunday was church and afternoon socials, but Harvey and I agreed to meet each other as soon as we each could get our bikes and check on the pond right away.

The day before—Saturday—had been the hottest day we could remember, and it had lasted all the way through the night. I had sweat and sweat and never really did get much sleep. This day had shaped up to be about the same. Both of us were already sweating bullets by the time we got to Old Man Grover's pasture, and Booney's tongue was hanging almost to the ground.

The first things we noticed were the cows. They were all huddled in a group at the top of the hill by the fence, some with their heads sticking through the barbed wire. Not eating grass or anything though, just looking like they wished they were someplace else. We looked down at what was left of the pond and then looked at each other in amazement. Our mouths were hanging open for the flies to buzz in and out as they pleased. Even Booney was just standing still beside me.

The water in the pond had receded enough that now it was just a puddle in the middle of a mud bog. And there in the middle of that mucky bit of water lay the exposed bones of some enormous beast.

It kind of looked like a dinosaur, or maybe a dragon because the bones didn't exactly fit any dinosaur we'd ever read about. And like most boys, we were crazy over dinosaurs, so we had quite a bit of knowledge in that area. The thing's spine curved up out of the mud, making a bow in the middle and sloping away at both ends. One end ran down into the muddy water and the other connected to something that looked like a big, misshapen bowling ball. It had to be the creature's skull. There were ridges of bone sticking up off the spine, bigger in the middle and running smaller at both ends. These were the things we had first seen and mistaken for fence posts. Even with all the moss and weeds and lily pads streaming down off the thing, it was an impressive sight.

It took us a long while to get up the courage to go down into the pasture and take a closer look, but of course, we finally did. It wasn't as big as it had looked from up on the hill, but it was still pretty big.

We walked around the muddy banks of the pond and looked at it from all angles. I called to Booney, but he wouldn't budge from the fence. I was all for running back to town and telling everybody what we had found, but Harvey just shook his head. "This is *our* monster, Stan," he said, with a funny gleam in his eye. "Vacation's over tomorrow and we gotta go back to school. Let's just enjoy him on our own, while we can."

Something about the way he said those things made me a little sad, I'm not sure why. But I could see why he didn't want to share the creature with anybody else just yet. I mean, we *had* put in all this time and worry over checking the pond every day.

He was right—it w*as* our monster. There'd be time enough to tell everyone later and I knew once word got out the whole pasture would fill up with gawkers and people taking pictures, probably scientists and maybe even the army or somebody. So, we just hiked a little ways back up the hill and fell back into the grass, laying there looking at our amazing discovery and every once in a while, taking sips of water from the canteen Harvey always wore on his belt. We talked about what kind of creature it could be. Harvey figured it was some kind of dinosaur that they hadn't gotten around to discovering yet, but I wasn't so sure. Something about the thing suggested more than just a giant reptile to me. I couldn't put my finger on it—still can't as a matter of fact—but my mind was spinning with all sorts of wild ideas. I told Harvey that I thought it was possible that this creature had come from outer space, Harvey looked down at it thoughtfully, then at me again. "Yeah," he said, "Why not?"

We stayed there until the stars came out and the crickets started singing. Even then we really didn't want to leave. But as I said—we suffered from overactive imaginations and there, in the dark, with the strange bones of that creature rising up out of the water, it was easy for us to work up a million scary scenes. So, we gathered up our bikes and began pedaling home with Booney running alongside as always. There was a refreshing breeze blowing and the temperature had dropped considerably.

Little did we know what that meant at the time.

We reached my driveway first and Booney and I said "so long" to Harvey, agreeing that tomorrow was going to be a humdinger of a day. We figured we'd be celebrities once we showed everybody the monster we found. I was excited, but also a little sad, remembering what Harvey had said about it being our monster. After tomorrow I guessed the monster would belong to everybody a little bit.

I stood on my pedals watching Harvey ride away into the night until he was just a speck in the moonlight, then laid on 'em and raced Booney up to the house. I got a little bit of a scolding from my mom about being out so late, but Dad took some of the load off by saying how it was pretty natural for a boy to use up every spare minute he could before his vacation was over and he had to go back to school. Dad was always real understanding about that sort of thing.

It was a long time before I finally drifted off to sleep that night. My mind wouldn't stop working thinking about all the ways those bones were going to make us famous. I imagined a parade in honor of Harvey and me, with confetti and a big marching band, and at the end a kiss right on the lips from Nancy Ann Wilson who was that year's County Dairy Princess. I saw us standing in front of the skeleton of that beast in some big museum, the bones now clean and gleaming white. Men with press cards in their hat bands snapped pictures of us. And the capper to the whole fantasy: the President of the United States stepping up to shake our hands!

My eyes finally grew heavy, and as I sank into sleep, I saw my curtains billow away from my open window with a sudden gust of wind and the last thing I heard was a pitter-patter across the roof like someone was throwing handfuls of gravel.

When I opened my eyes the next morning that pitter-patter had increased to a sound more like an army marching across our rooftop. I looked out my window and saw nothing but a sheet of water pouring out of a mean, gray sky. The window was shut now, and I knew that my ma had come into the room during the night to close it. There were droplets of water on the floor underneath it.

I got up and walked over to the window, not quite believing what I saw. The trees were whipping around in the wind and the rain was coming down relentlessly. Not straight down either, but sort of sideways, especially when the wind tore through with a really strong gust. Our driveway was all mud and there were big soggy puddles all over our yard.

I wandered downstairs to get my breakfast and met my dad in the kitchen. He looked at me over his newspaper, arched his eyebrows, and said, "Guess our early summer is over, eh?"

I agreed and sat down to a plateful of scrambled eggs and toast that Mom had gotten ready for me. My dad told me he would take me to school that day so I wouldn't get drowned or blown away; normally I rode my bike.

All day at school, I sat in the classrooms and watched the world drowning outside. The rain never did let up if anything it came down harder. I sat with Harvey at lunch, and we ate our bologna sandwiches and talked quietly about what we knew was going on out in Old Man Grover's pasture. We had decided not to mention what we had found to anybody until after we'd had a chance to get back out there and see for ourselves.

I don't think a week has ever dragged by as slowly as that one did. The previous week of waiting for the sun to dry up that pond was nothing compared to that solid week of rain. All Harvey and I could do was sit inside our houses and wonder what was happening to our amazing discovery. But finally, of course, the rain did stop, and our folks once again allowed us to roam free. Our first attempt at getting out to that pasture was thwarted by the river flooding over and washing out the only road that went out that way. That meant leaving our bikes and hiking out through the woods on foot. That was pretty far out of our way, but we were mighty determined so on Saturday we packed up a couple of lunches and filled up

Harvey's canteen and trekked on out there. Booney followed along, of course; he didn't mind the walk at all.

The heat was coming back, and you could see the trees steaming as the sun hit them. The ground beneath our feet was spongy, but the woods were on high land, so our feet only got a little soggy. It was a pretty fine trip; the day was warm and bright, and I had my two best friends in the world along with me. By the time we stepped out of the woods, we were laughing so hard our stomachs hurt and even Booney had that silly grin he always got when Harvey and I got the giggles.

The laughter stopped though, as we came out of the trees and stared down into the valley.

It was completely flooded.

The only ground to be seen was one lone island close to the middle of what was now a lake, with two sick-looking cows lying on it. There was no sign of our monster. You couldn't even tell where the pond had originally been.

Harvey threw his backpack on the ground and then sat down hard, his face turning red and the tears welling up in his eyes. I knew how he felt. We could tell as many people as we wanted that there were monster bones down in that valley, but there was no way anyone would believe us now.

Harvey looked up at me after a minute and said: "How long did it take for that pond to go down enough that we could see them bones, Stan?"

I knew what he was thinking. "All of our lives," I said.

"The heat spell was just luck," he said. "It might not ever happen again, especially now that the darn valley's turned into a lake. The only way to see that monster now is to take a submarine down there."

"Maybe you could swim it," I said, but not really with any confidence. No one had ever gone swimming in that mucky little pond before. I looked down into the water that filled the valley and shuddered to think of all the snakes and leeches that lurked in that brown and green lake.

“Nobody'd believe us," Harvey said quietly. No, no one would.

Harvey moved away a couple years after that. I missed him terribly—still do in fact, I never did have another friend quite like him; do you know what I mean? You probably do.

Anyway, he and I would occasionally go down to what used to be Old Man Grover's pasture, coming home from fishing or something. We'd just kind of swing out that way without really thinking or talking about it. The water receded some, but never quite enough for us to tell if it was pond-size again. We just couldn't seem to remember how it originally was. After a while, we just gave it up and stopped going out that way. Then Harvey moved and I started high school and got all sorts of other things to think about. That day we saw the monster bones seemed a million years behind me.

Or like a dream.

Last spring, I took my wife and daughter to see the town where I grew up. It hasn't really changed compared to some places I've seen. It's a little bigger - three traffic lights now, instead of one - and the drug store is gone, replaced by a market chain that doesn't even sell comic books on that squeaky, wobbly, rotating rack. But like I said, mostly it's the same. The people are still friendly and the clock on the courthouse still keeps time.

My daughter being something of a tomboy, I decided to take her fishing along the river. We went to one of our old "secret fishin' holes." It was almost like stepping back in time, so little had changed about it. The cut of the river might have been a little different, but imperceptibly so. Another thing that hadn't changed was my luck. My daughter, Sarah, caught two nice-looking brook trout. I walked away empty-handed.

As we were driving back into town, I recognized one of the fields and it all came flooding back. I pulled the car over onto the gravel that edged the road and slowly came to a stop. I told Sarah I wanted to walk up the hill and take a look down into the valley. I told her I remembered a pond that my best friend and I used to play around. That's all I told her.

We got out of the car and started walking through the tall, brown grass. Off to my right a little, I could see the hill that Harvey and I had rolled down that first day we saw the "fence posts." The day was warm and sunny, and bits of dandelion fluff floated on the breeze. I could almost see ol' Booney trotting along beside me.

When we reached the top of the rise, I stopped to get my breath back—but it wouldn't come. I stared down into the valley and just couldn't believe what I was seeing.

A housing development was in the process of being constructed.

The woods on the far side—where Harvey and I had come out that day after it stopped raining—were partially cut back and the slope of the hills was exposed. It looked slightly obscene to me somehow, all that naked space. Foundations were set in places, and the skeletons of walls were even set up in some of them. A couple of big caterpillars and a dump truck sat silently waiting for the next day's work. But the thing that wouldn't let me get my breath back was this: the pond wasn't there anymore. And neither was our monster.

I considered for a moment that maybe I was mistaken about the location. No, the hills surrounding the valley were too well embedded in my memory. Was it possible they had somehow drained the pond? But then, what had happened to the bones?

Eventually, I took Sarah by the hand and wandered back to the car. She wanted to know what the big deal had been. I didn't know what to tell her, except that sometimes changes came where you least expected them.

I didn't let myself think about the implications of that housing development until after we'd been home a few days. I guess I was acting strangely, because my wife called me to dinner one night by saying, "Earth to Stan, Earth to Stan, come in Stan."

I toyed with the idea of trying to locate Harvey again, after all these years. He was really the only one I could talk to. But it had been so long, and the memories I had of the days when we were best friends had become so treasured that I couldn't bear to have the reality of adulthood tarnish them. So, I never did. In time, just like when I was a kid, I was able to put it away in a closet in the back of my mind and get on with life.

But, of course, I still take out those memories and dust them off every once in a while. In those memories, Harvey and I ride our bikes down dusty roads, drink sodas and read comic books at the drugstore, and sit on that big rock with our fishin' poles in the water, not catching anything, and not caring. And in every memory, Booney's there to chase us down, wherever we're headed.

I wonder about those monstrous bones and what happened to them. I wonder how they came to be there in the first place. I remember sitting in that pasture and gazing on that marvelous monster, burning its image into my mind, talking about where it came from. I remember telling Harvey that I thought it might be a visitor from outer space, somehow fallen to Earth. I remember what Harvey said to that.

Did the creature's own kind come back to Earth and reclaim its long-lost bones? Did those bones just get up by themselves and walk away? Did Harvey figure out a way to remove them without letting anyone know, or did they just sink further into the ground, disappearing from everyone's sight?

I guess I'll never know for sure, but the possibilities are intriguing.

Why not? That was the answer Harvey gave me, and I can still hear his voice, summing up every fantastic, unexplainable moment of my childhood. Summing up every fantastic, unexplainable moment yet to come.

Why not?

Scott West is a writer/musician currently living in the Pacific Northwest.

Made in the USA
Columbia, SC
18 April 2024

34604340R00120